D1479026

DISCARD

Murda Season 2

Lock Down Publications and Ca$h
Presents

Murda Season 2

A Novel by *Romell Tukes*

Lock Down Publications
P.O. Box 944
Stockbridge, Ga 30281
www.lockdownpublications.com

Copyright 2020 Romell Tukes
Murda Season 2

All rights reserved. No part of this book may be reproduced in any form or by electronic or mechanical means, including information storage and retrieval systems without permission in writing from the publisher, except by a reviewer who may quote brief passages in review.
First Edition November 2020
Printed in the United States of America

This is a work of fiction. Names, characters, places, and incidents either are products of the author's imagination or are used fictitiously. Any similarity to actual events or locales or persons, living or dead, is entirely coincidental.

Lock Down Publications
Like our page on Facebook: Lock Down Publications @ www.facebook.com/lockdownpublications.ldp
Cover design and layout by: **Dynasty Cover Me**
Book interior design by: **Shawn Walker**
Edited by: **Leondra Williams**

Stay Connected with Us!

Text **LOCKDOWN** to 22828 to stay up-to-date with new releases, sneak peaks, contests and more…

Thank you!

Submission Guideline.

Submit the first three chapters of your completed manuscript to ldpsubmissions@gmail.com, subject line: Your book's title. The manuscript must be in a .doc file and sent as an attachment. Document should be in Times New Roman, double spaced and in size 12 font. Also, provide your synopsis and full contact information. If sending multiple submissions, they must each be in a separate email.

Have a story but no way to send it electronically? You can still submit to LDP/Ca$h Presents. Send in the first three chapters, written or typed, of your completed manuscript to:

LDP: Submissions Dept
P.O. Box 944
Stockbridge, Ga 30281

DO NOT send original manuscript. Must be a duplicate.

Provide your synopsis and a cover letter containing your full contact information.

Thanks for considering LDP and Ca$h Presents.

Acknowledgements

First and foremost, all praises are due to Allah. I want to thank my family peeps, sisters and day ones for the support and loyalty. You know who you are. Shout out to my Peeky family, Took, Killer, Naya, Berty, BA and the whole city for their support. My Yankers fam Spayhoe, Smurf, Fresh, CB, YB, Baby James, Berger, and my brother Snake Black, 358. My Newberry nigga Spice, Dable, O, Bogo, Black, and Lil Bam. My BX crew, Free Melly, Hump, BJ, P.God, Menkey, Fatal, and A-1. My Beckly team Tim Dog, OG ChuckK, from Thompkings, Official East New York, Big Will, DayDay from Crown Heights and of course Tails free the guys. My Paterson niggas and my Muscle gang Fitness crew. Follow your dreams. Shout to the LDP family who work extra hard to take over the game. Stay tuned! It's a movie.

Chapter One

Connecticut Lake, CT

Murda and Tookie were seated at the glass table on the upper deck of the 2.3-million-dollar yacht that belonged to Web. It was a bright, hot beautiful day on the crystal-clear water lake that connected from Long Island to Connecticut.

"Mr. Saukanav please, tell me you have good news for me and my father. By the way, my father sends his apology for not being present at this meeting," Murda said to the Italian man sitting across from him in gray Salvaterra Ferragamo suit.

"Somewhat Murda, you see Joe is a very smart man. It's been a year since Freddy died, murdered by the hands of your people so he is very suspicious and skeptical of everybody around him," Saukanav stated blowing cigar smoke out his mouth.

"What do you have for me?" Murda questioned, getting frustrated.

Mr. Saukhanav was a close associate to Joe. They grew up together and he worked for Joe as a hitman.

When Saukanav found out Joe was fucking his wife and daughter, he went to Web offering his assistant as a helper in Joe's circle for two hundred dollars a month.

"His nephew, Sergio just came home from beating five bodies in the fields but he still did twenty-years for putting two hits on the pigs in Boston. He's in New York and Joe gave him Freddy's old position as the capo of the family. Listen, this fucker is dangerous," he said making Tookie laugh.

"Sergio, huh? Ok what else you got for me?" Murda asked looking at his $327,000 Auchena Piguet watch under the sleeve of his Givenchy blazer.

"This is Joe's daughter Miley's address. She lives in Plainfield, New Jersey." Saukanav slid Murda a piece of paper.

"Good work," Murda said rubbing his five o'clock shadow beard.

"So, when do I get paid for this month's work?" Saukanav inquired, thinking about spending half of his pay on hookers.

"About that. I don't think we need your assistance no more. No offense but I just don't trust white people, especially after what y'all did to Emmett Till," Murda stated.

"Wait, what happened to our agreement?" he replied with fire in his voice.

"Sometimes agreements are only made to be broken," Murda stated sounding like his father

Murda pulled out a gun and shot the Italian four times in the face, then Tookie grabbed the man's lifeless bloody body and tossed him into the lake.

When Murda heard the hard splash, he popped a 15-liter bottle of Armand De Brignac worth $50,000

"Since when you become a drinker blood?" Tookie asked seeing Murda pour himself a drink.

"Since I turned twenty-one four months ago, but me and pops was talking. It's time we come out of our caves. It's been a year. I'm gonna call Live can only do so much. But first we gotta get these noddle eating pigs out the way son," Murda said as Tookie nodded, ready to turn up.

After Tookie's little brother YB was murdered by Stacks, he hadn't been the same. All he saw was blood. Even after Murda told him that YB was killed for stealing from Stacks. Murda let him know that he bodied Stacks for him.

Today, Murda was on a new level. He was a young boss under his father's guidance and Tookie was his muscle.

He chose to give his little brother, Gunna a position within the empire because after he was shot and ended his basketball career, he turned into a savage in Brooklyn. He was already making a serious name for himself.

"You want me to handle that nigga Sergio?" asked Rookie.

There were five bad ass Spanish bitches downstairs from Washington Heights. They were sleep from the crazy rendezvous they had hours ago with both men.

"No, just play the background. Let Gunna and Live handle it they gotta earn their bones in this game," Murda said hoping his little brother could perform well under pressure.

"Aight fam, but what's popping with Joe's daughter?"

"Oh, I'ma pay her a visit myself, just to let Joe know that we're back in town," Murda said smiling walking downstairs to toss the five bitches in the lake, just in case any of them heard the gunshots. He trusted no bitch.

"I hope them bitches can swim," Tookie laughed, following Murda downstairs already knowing what they were about to do.

*****

Bridgeport, CT.

Rick Ross' album was booming on the stereo throughout the garage area that looked like a real gym.

With flat benches, free weights, dumbbell, rack, kettles balls, universal machines, squat racks, pull up bars, clip bars, treadmills, bicycles, and a juice bar, this was better than Gold's gym.

Web was under the incline bench lifting two hundred seventy-five pounds of free weights pig iron by himself

"Twenty," he said with a grit hanging the heavy weight on the rack for his last set.

Web walked over to a mat and started doing burpee's with push-ups, dripping in sweat with his shirt off showing his chiseled six pack and defined chest and arms.

For a nigga just turning forty, Web looked better than any nigga in his twenties. His strict diet of no meat and six days a week exercise routine was to thank for that.

After his ninety minutes of weight training and cardio, he went for his daily swim in his backyard.

The mansion was a glass house mansion in a gated rich community, where he had twenty-four seven security guards with licenses to carry and kill.

The palace had ten bedrooms, six bathrooms, 8,751 square feet, upstairs and downstairs, game room, movie theater, custom made wallpaper from caline, mink rugs throughout the house, a guest house, a lake in the back with a dock for his yacht, and manicured clean cut grass throughout the acres.

It had been a year and some change since Web showed his face in New York. He needed to fall back and regroup. Especially after finding out his wife Carmilla was a federal agent who was also the daughter of his connect, Rafael.

When Rafael last spoke to Web, he informed him he killed his father Jose Rodriguez years ago. After hearing that, it was war, but Web needed time to plan correctly without losing everything he worked so hard for all his life.

After his right-hand man Stacks was murdered by his son, Murda, he needed a new crew of muscles to still run the streets and his business operation.

Luckily, Murda stepped up with our team and they were hatching shit down with a new Venezuelan connect he had met on a trip to Brazil with his son last year.

Murda was still playing the background while he let Gunna flood the street with the bricks. Web felt it was time to handle his unfinish affairs. His clubs, restaurants, and stores were all still up and running and doing well while he let his co-partners run his business operations.

Web saw his yacht coming on the lake as he climbed out the pool, looking at his wedding ring he still wore for a reason he could never figure out.

Every time he saw Murda and Tookie together, it reminded him of him and Stacks when they first came in the game.

Web was really upset his son killed his best friend, but he blamed himself because he should have told Murda years ago he was his father, but he didn't feel it was the correct timing.

He been keeping tabs on him and his daughter, Ariana who was overseas in the army. Soon, he planned to approach her but right now he was focused on placing his crown back on his head.

Chapter Two

Washington, D.C.

Carmilla was sitting in her office in the D.C. federal building, two blocks away from the White House.

She was looking at a thick file of a mob boss in New York named Joe. He had four federal cases in the last twenty years.

For this case to get to the headquarters in D.C., it had to be major like John Gotti's case.

Looking through the photos, she could tell the old man was from Brooklyn. She was a little familiar with the area when she was living in New York with Web.

Carmilla stopped what she was doing and took off her Versace glasses, leaning back in her chair looking out her office window.

Every time she thought of New York, the only person she could think about was Web. He was the only man she loved. She knew what she did was wrong by trying to build a federal case on him because her evil father made her do it.

When she fell in love with him, she was trying to do everything in her power to prolong the case, but her boss was on her back. He thought he had something big, but her father was smart enough to clean his trails with Web while "setting him up."

When Web kidnapped her, she feared for her life, but she knew if Web wanted her dead after finding out she was an agent, she would be been dead.

Luckily, she was able to run away and get free, but the event left her mentally and emotional disturbed.

She still wore her wedding ring on her every day, because it was the only memory she had of the man who filled her dreams.

It was like Web disappeared from the planet and his case.

One day, her boss told her to dismiss any evidence or material she had on Web and it was from the higher ups.

Carmilla knew it had to be some foul play or somebody knew somebody in very high power to just dismiss a high-profile case such as Web's.

That was perfect for Carmilla because she was trying to withhold everything she had anyway to protect him, so it all worked in her favor.

Her boss told her she would have to go to New York for a while, which was hard for her because of what happened last time. Carmilla told nobody about her being kidnapped for up to four months. She told her boss she was on an emergency vacation because she was sick with bad flu.

Carmilla grabbed her Chanel purse, and prepared to go out to eat lunch in her blouse and Chanel pen skirt and six-inch heels.

*****

East New York, Brooklyn

Gunna Da Don and Live were twenty deep at the biggest basketball tournament in the city of their hometown.

"You cross that nigga son," Gunna yelled in front of the large crowd on the bleachers near the sideline.

One of the players who had the ball was halfway down the court dribbling the ball. The nigga went left on his opponent playing defense on him, then he faked went right, and hit him with a spin move. He then side stepped him, backing up making his opponent fall on the floor, twisting his ankle in the process, causing the crowd to go crazy.

The basketball player then moved into the box, crossing over two more niggas then slam dunked the ball, causing the whole park go bananas. They went bonkers

"Ohhhh!" Gunna was jumping up and down as the game was over. He had $100,000 on the game with his man Skrap from Fort Green projects.

Gunna Da Don is what the hood called him now. He was once known as the best basketball player in Brooklyn until Trap shot him up, almost killing him. Unfortunately for Gunna, the bullets fucked his ACL up so bad, the doctor thought he would never be able to walk again.

After being shot, Gunna made a choice to say fuck school and focus on the street life.

Murda wasn't too happy, but he couldn't do nothing about it, except show him how to do it right and get money.

It just so happened, his best friend Live was fresh home from his state bid in Bea Hill prison upstate and he was with Gunna every step of the way.

Both men were raw, only nineteen-years-old, living the life grown men dreamed of. They had Brooklyn on lock. Every hood and gang was fucking with Gunna and Live.

"Yo blood, we gotta go holler at Loon and them niggas, son. Bay on parole and it's getting late," Live said as the streetlights came on as the sky darkened.

Gunna was talking to two thick black chicks who wore booty shorts and belly shirts showing off their flat abs and curves.

Gunna had on two Jesus pieces diamond chains, a Rolex lost dawn chemical encrusted watch, bracelets, and diamond earrings.

"Aight, Bay, we out. I'ma call y'all later. Keep it tight," Gunna said walking off

"Okay, we will, Gunna Da Don," one of the black chicks said, blowing bubbles from her gum through her thick juicy lips.

As they were walking out the crowded park, their soldiers were less than ten feet behind them.

"Live, my brother said he gotta holler at us about something tomorrow and to meet him under the Brooklyn bridge," Gunna stated.

"He coming to the town?" Live asked, shock because normally they would meet him in Connecticut or Port Chester in Westchester to re-up.

"Facts son," Gunna said climbing in his all red BMW M2 two door. All of their goons had fast luxury cars, as well as designer clothes

Live pulled off first, speeding down the block with a desert eagle in his lap, listening to Styles P. Live was from Cypress

Projects next to the Pink Houses where Gunna and Murda were from. Live grew up in the streets. His mother and father were Muslims who owed a Mosque in downtown Brooklyn.

He was a Muslim also, but he grew up gangbanging under Murda's set and running the streets day and night.

At sixteen, Live caught an attempted murder charge and was set up north for three years. Luckily, it was his first charge, or he would have been hit with ten years or more.

He spent his time reading, rapping, exercising on the pull up bar and kicking it with old heads from his block up top with him schooling him.

Gunna was the only nigga sending him money, pics, and letters as well as his big homie, Murda. He came home six-foot, weight up, waves, chipped tooth and focused on a bag. He was black as night, but the ladies loved his dark, smooth African skin, courtesy of his Botswanan parents.

Since he came home last year, shit been good. He couldn't believe how fast his life changed, thanks to Gunna.

Chapter Three

Brooklyn Bridge

Gunna and Live both sat under the Brooklyn Bridge in the dark, inside of a black Maserati Granturismo sport car with tints, looking at the bright light skyscrapers, giving the city that New York skyline look.

"You good bro?" Live asked Gunna who was staring off into the sky.

"I'm straight, you heard. Lil Kobe texted me saying he shot CJ," Gunna said looking at his phone to see a text from his wife Nikki. She was texting him her location, so he could come smash..

"He'll be alright," Live said lighting a blunt of granddaddy Kush.

"Here they go right here, B. Pass me that blunt real quick, boy."

Live passed him the blunt and looked at the three pairs of headlights behind them as they climbed out the car both rocking Balmain sweatshirts.

*****

Murda pulled up in a robot white, Rolls Royce Ghost followed by two Escalade SUV trucks fill of gunmen under Murda's command.

This was Murda's first time back Brooklyn since he killed Stacks. That was also the same night he was tasered and put to sleep by Web's goons.

Murda hopped out the Ghost, like a true boss in a Marc Jacob suit walking towards his little brother and Live, with a yellow folder in his hand.

"Niggas still wearing sweat suits. Y'all gotta step y'all shit up with all that money y'all making," Murda said, as he embraced both men.

"This Balmain blood is a stack or better type shit. I see you on your Mr. Rodger's shit," Gonna said as him and Live laughed.

"You got that son, but look peep game bro. Me and my pops coming back on the scene. We still going to have a low profile and you still got the streets. We focus on businesses."

"That's what's popping," said Gunna, happy big bro was back on the scene.

"Welcome back son," Live stated

"That's the good news but the bad news is we coming back to finish some unwanted beef with the Mafia," Murda said as Gunna and Live looked at each other

"I think I've heard about that shit. It used to be all over the news. That was you?" Gunna asked.

"Yeah but a lot comes with money and fame. One of them things is murder and it's the right season for it," Murda smiled.

"Aight who?" Live asked

"This is everything y'all need to know about him but take your time. This is a new level. The drug game and murder game are two different fields," Murda stated, waving the folder in the air.

"We both killed before, Jamel. We know what to do and how to do it," Gunna said ticking the folder with an attitude because he felt like his brother was trying to play him.

"Fucking listen, that's your problem. These aren't regular street niggas. These are official killers who will kill everything, including you. Once they find out we're related to Web, we just as good as dead." Murda all about the beef with the MCB and Rafael so he was on point and wanted his brother to be safe also.

"We going to take care of it, bro. Just give us some time."

"Say less, son. If y'all need anything, holler at me or Tookie."

"When the next shipment?" Gunna asked.

"Sunday. The cargo is going to be in Manhattan. It's going to be the same routine. I'm not gotta wake up a lying dog to let him know the apes are back in town for blood," Murda said walking off.

*****

Plainfield, NJ

Murda parked the Escalade truck on the side block of the dark quiet suburb neighborhood that reminded him of Nightmare on Elm Street.

He came alone as he looked at the brick house with the large white door and a porch with the night light on.

This was the home of Miley, one of many of Joe's children and tonight he was going to send a message. Joe didn't know Murda or who he was but tonight he was going to make sure he did.

There was a navy-blue Acura RDX truck parked in the driveway. He wondered if she was married, had a boyfriend or if there was anybody else in the house he had to be wary of.

Murda hopped out in an all-black Champion sweat suit, with a pistol in his hoodie pocket.

He walked towards the backyard to avoid noisy neighbors. Luckily, there was no dogs because he hated dogs.

Her grass was high as if she ain't cut it in months, as he made it to her back porch to see glass slider doors.

Like magic, when he pulled the latch, it opened, as he shook his head. This had to be a white neighborhood because no black was leaving no doors unlock in the hood. Niggas was even locking windows on the seventeenth floor, as if a nigga can climb in.

Once inside the tile floor kitchen, he heard loud moans as if someone was fucking in the next room.

Murda looked around the corner towards the living holding on to the kitchen doorway hall to see a sexy ass naked woman using a big black vibrator while watching a black porn movie.

*****

Miley was a middle school gym teacher at twenty-seven. She was Joe's youngest, his baby girl.

She was single, no kids, and she had her own shit. She was obsessed with blacks and if her father knew, he would kill her or at least cut her off for life.

Miley was five foot five, blue and green eyes, petite, big DD breast, long curly dirty blonde hair, thin lips, big long pointy nose with a round perfect ass for her size.

She knew her father was a mobster. Growing up in Brooklyn was hard because he was so busy. He paid her no mind even when her mom died in an airplane crash when she was ten. Miley went to college at Texas A & M and moved to New Jersey and became a schoolteacher and kept a low-profile life.

She had her fair share of black men, but all wanted to tell her she was just a little too crazy. She only had sexual desires for blacks. This is why she never been with a white guy.

"Ugh…yes fuck this tight pussy with that big black cock," she screamed, ramming the twelve-inch vibrator in her wet pussy, while talking to the porn on her TV screen. "Fuck me harder," she said putting the vibrator in and out her pussy as cum coated the toy.

"Take your time," a voice said from behind her as she froze, staring at Murda and his swollen dick print.

"If you're going to kill me, at least let me finish" she said shoving her sex toy so deep in her pussy, it almost disappeared as she moaned loudly putting on a show for him.

Murda couldn't believe what he was seeing. Miley's pussy was so phat, it looked like it was having an allergic reaction.

"Ugh, mmmmm. I'm about to cum. Let me suck your dick. I'll cum hard," she said, giving him a sexy look as cum started to pour out her pussy while her legs started to shake.

Boc.

Boc.

Boc.

Boc.

Boc.

Murda had to hurry and kill her because he was about to put his dick in her mouth.

Miley was slumped on her couch with holes in her chest and one hand on her big black vibrator that was still in her pussy.

Murda left the porn movie on as he walked out the same way he came in. He was fucked up at the sight he just saw. There was no doubt in his mind that Miley was a cold-blooded freak and she died with honor.

Chapter Four

Las Vegas, NV

Chelsea was sitting at a blackjack card table alone, in a red Saint Laurent slit dress showing her perfect figure.

Chelsea changed her appearance. She changed her blonde hair to a dark red color to give her exotic blue eyes and beautiful face more sex appeal.

She moved to Vegas last year after her two children were murdered by Freddy, because of her husband Chris' debt he owed the mafia.

After losing her two daughters, her heart turned ice cold. So cold she killed her husband Chris. She watched as two killer wild hogs ate his flesh to the bone.

Little did she know, Joe had her kids killed because he found out Chris was Web's brother and he wanted to send a message.

Chelsea ran to Italy with her father Donvito, who was the biggest mob boss in the world. Her father owned a shore of casino's in Vegas with other MOB families, so he sent his daughter to watch over his casinos and network.

"Excuse me, beautiful lady. May I join you?" A handsome brown skin man with a low Caesar cut, perfect white teeth, dimples, hazel eyes, tall, lean build, and dressed in a Dior for men suit, stood next to her and asked.

"Sure," Chelsea said sipping Moet out of her glass, leaving red lipstick on the rim.

"Dealer, can you please deal me in?" the man requested, placing ten grand worth of poker chips on the table.

"If the lady agrees," the dealer replied who was an old white man.

"It's cool," Chelsea stated looking over at him stare at her smiling.

"I'm Ralph from LA," the man said introducing himself.

"I'm Lauren, nice to meet you," Chelsea lied, coming up with the first name to come to mind.

"Ralph and Lauren, the perfect couple," he said. As the dealer laid cards on the table, he tried to give the man look trying to tell him to just leave.

"Yeah, perfect. So, Ralph, where is your wife? I'm sure a handsome man such as yourself isn't alone."

"Actually I am. I came out to enjoy myself. What happens in Vegas, stays in Vegas."

"I agree so why waste time," she said looking at him sexually as he lost his blackjack hand. He wasn't upset because he was a big-time drug dealer in Watts and he was also a Grape Street Crip with his own set.

"I'm waiting on your move beautiful," he said. Chelsea stood up and grabbed his smooth hand so he could follow her.

The elevator ride was quiet to the penthouse floor. When they got off on the last floor, there was two big white men in suits standing at the double with their arms crossed.

Once inside the penthouse, Ralph was amazed at how big it was. The room contained marble floors, marble ceilings, wall to wall carpet, Versace furniture, tables made by French designers and an inside bar.

"This shit is fly," he said looking around as she took off her heels and tossed her purse on the couch.

"Thank you but come to the room. I hope you can perform as well as you can talk," she said, starting to the upstairs master bedroom.

"I will," he said looking at her nice round ass bounce with every step as his dick grew.

As soon as they entered the room, Ralph took off his clothes getting naked showing his six pack and Crip tattoo's all over his body, which turned her on.

When she saw his big hard ten inch black dick, her pussy got soaked.

Chelsea took off her dress. She was wearing no panties or bra as Ralph stared at a phat, small, pretty shaved pussy and nice C cup breast. She had a work-out body with abs.

"Damn you sexy," he said sitting on the bed as she got on her knees.

"I know," Chelsea responded licking the tip of his dick slowly, then working her way to the bottom engulfing all ten inches with no gagging.

"Uhmm shiitt," he moaned as his eyes rolled in the back of his head. He tightened his face as she bopped her head up and down on his dick while rubbing his balls.

"Feel good?" she asked, twisting her head on the tip of his dick while sucking up his pre-cum then spitting back on his dick, throwing it down her throat.

She swallowed every drop of semen and rubbed his dick all over her face as she got cum in her ponytail.

"What the fuck," he said coming back to life never experiencing a head game like that.

Ralph laid her on the bed and threw her legs over his shoulders as she widened her legs and raised her hips higher so he could get deep in her as she like it. Chelsea let out a soft moan as he slowly entered her wet pussy that felt like warm water as he started to slicken her pussy.

"Yes," she whispered in a moan, as she squeezed the bed sheets as he was sliding in and out her throbbing pussy. She thrusted her hips upward as he rammed his big dick in her tight pussy.

"You like this black dick bitch?"

"Ugh, yes fuck-k me," she yelled as he went deeper and harder, soaking his dick with her thick cum as she finally climaxed.

Their moans and groans filled the room as they were going as it like wild animals. He flipped her on her stomach for the next round. His dick was still standing strong ready for war.

Chelsea laid on her stomach and spread her legs wide open while placing her ass in the air, giving him a full view of her pussy lip and pink little asshole that looked so tight, a finger couldn't fit inside.

Ralph spread her soft ass cheek and went to work as he started to tear her ass up as he was hitting her g-spot and banging her walls down.

"Ugh I'm cumming," she cried as cum squirted out on his dick. Her pussy got sloppy wet as he nutted seconds later, tired and worn out.

Chelsea was now in her freak zone. She wrapped her lips around his dick sucking her cum off of it, loving the taste.

She climbed on his dick and began to ride in a reverse cowgirl, making her ass clap on his dick as if she was a stripper.

"Oh shit, fuck," he gritted, feeling her pussy walls tighten around his dick squeezing it for dear life. She had him on the verge of busting another nut.

After ten minutes of riding, the two came at the same time and fell asleep. Ralph wanted to take her back to LA. She was the best fuck he ever had. He was in love with her drip.

Two hours later, Chelsea woke up and quietly got dressed while Ralph was sleeping. Chelsea walked out the penthouse in her red dress and heels to see her guards still posted

"Kill him and get rid of the body and this time dispose the whole body. Thank you," Chelsea said walking off as the guards went in the penthouse to kill Ralph. This was one of the many times they had to do this for their boss. They felt sad for whoever got a piece of her pussy because it would be there last.

Chapter Five

New Jersey Turnpike

Sergio was driving in his fast forest green new Audi R8 V10 plus, speeding through traffic heading back to Brooklyn to speak with his boss Joe who said he needs to speak to him.

Sergio was Joe's younger cousin who was raised in Boston. He grew up into the Mafia and it wasn't easy in Boston because the Irish MCB run the city.

There was a big war with Sergio and the Irish Mafia and Sergio killed all of their top leaders, coming out on top.

Not too long after the war died down, the Feds arrested Sergio and forty-six others in his camp.

Sergio beat five murders at trial but was charged with drug trafficking, the R.I.C.O, and money fraud, which landed him in prison for twenty years.

Since he been home, he moved to New York and opened a couple of legit businesses and became Joe's capo.

At forty-four, he was well put together and worked-out daily. He didn't smoke or drink, no kids, no wife and he loved sex with dancers and hookers.

With his parents gone years ago, the only family members he had was a brother and sister, who were both younger than him, but they all were on bad terms.

He was a short man with short man complex, a baldhead, a goatee, tattoos on his head from prison, and a muscular built.

Sergio was a fashion freak. He loved suits and fancy cars. He had a very expensive taste for the finer things in life especially after being in prison for twenty years.

*****

An hour later

Brooklyn

Joe sat in his office in the back of his tailor-made suit store on Cart St. staring at the roses, with the small letter attached to it.

Life had been good for the mob boss since Web been out the picture. He spent the last year and the year before warring with Web every season. He lost a lot of friends, family, and money fucking beefing with a man he never even saw face to face, yet Web was like a killer ghost to him.

There wasn't a day that went by that Joe didn't look over his shoulder for Web, but he got too comfortable until now.

When he heard from his brother who worked on Wall St. that Miley was murdered last week, he lost it.

He kept Miley in New Jersey for this reason, to make sure she was safe now she was gone, and he felt like it was his fault.

Hearing she died while masturbating to black porn disgusted him but that was still his baby girl.

Today, when Joe came in, he saw roses with a letter attached to it. When he read it, his heart stopped.

The letter read, *I'm back. Hope you liked my welcome back gift. Your daughter is a freak but see you soon xoxo.*

He was waiting on Sergio to arrive so he could inform him of what was going on and how it was time for a war with the blacks again.

Sergio walked in minutes later with has bop.

"Boss man," Sergio said, seeing the awkward look on Joe's face, as he sat behind his desk staring at the flowers still wrapped up nice and neatly.

"Sit down."

"Everything okay?" Sergio asked sincerely concerned.

"No. I found out who killed my daughter."

"Who?"

"That motherfucking nigger, Web," Joe shouted slamming his fist into his desk.

Sergio heard of the famous Web many times. Some say he was a deadly ghost with so much money, he could own half of Brooklyn.

When he was in the Feds, he heard every Brooklyn nigga speak about Web as if he was some type of legend.

"So, what are we going to do?" Sergio asked already knowing his answer.

"Get ready for a war with these cock suckers. I know he is going show his face, especially after I had his little family killed. I only wished I could have killed his brother, Chris the Federal agent but someone beat me to the punch and did a good job I must say."

"I'ma get a man on it ASAP," Sergio said standing up.

"Don't sleep on him. Something is telling me he's not back alone. This is from a message say, I know how bosses move because I am a boss," Joe said before Sergio left not trying to hear him brag.

*****

Colanta, Colombia

Rafael sat in his garden under the gazebo in the yard of his mansion, sipping on freshly squeezed orange juice.

The weather was hot, sticky, and humid as if it was about to rain outside today.

He was dressed in a custom-made tux from his personal tailor, waiting on his meeting with a future client from the UK who dealt with large amounts of coke.

Things been somewhat rough for the Colombian Cartel boss because he found out he had a liver disease. He was now confined to an oxygen machine since his lungs were badly damaged.

Web stayed on his mind daily. It was as if the men went to hid in an underground tunnel somewhere, which made him nervous.

A person will never know what a man like Web is up to because he was very discreet and wise.

Rafael felt like giving him to the Feds was a checkmate move but he had no clue Carmilla will fall in love with him, which destroyed all his plans because he wasn't able to connect the dots.

Now his life and Carmilla's, was on the line with a very dangerous man. Rafael could never forget the day he killed Web's father. That's why he played him so close.

*****

Barahona, Dominican Republic
Twenty-Four Years Ago...

Jose had just walked into his ranch style house in a rush, coming back from the states from spending time with his son Webster.

Jose was a handsome Dominican man, tall, tan, hazel eyes, lean, curly hair, and soft spoken. He was raised in New York, but DR was his home and birthplace.

He was a drug lord and very connected with a lot of powerful men across the world.

As soon as he got to his bedroom, he seen a man sitting on his bed with a gun in his lap.

"Rafael, what the fuck," Jose said scared, as his heart was racing from the man he was trying to get away from.

Jose came home to pack up and move out his country before Rafael came looking for him because word was, he wanted him dead because he found a new connect.

"You in a rush, Joe," Rafael said in Spanish.

"No, not at all. What are you doing here, my friend?" Jose asked in Spanish.

"I hear you got a new connect and you still owe me money from the four thousand kilos you got on consignment," Rafael stated.

"I have your money, papi. It's downstairs."

"Good, good. But we been doing business for a long time now and you never crossed me until now. I want to who it is."

"When you cross me, I won't let you do it again," Rafael said shooting him eight times in the face, leaving him dead on the bedroom floor.

Rafael heard his guest come out the back as his guard approached him. He took Web off his mind and focused on business. He was most likely dead somewhere by now.

Rafael was training his son to take over the family business and he was catching on very fast he had potential.

Chapter Six

White Plains, N.Y.

"Jamika, I'm giving this case to you. Don't fuck it up and be careful because you're dealing with the Mafia now, and their smart. If you need a partner, I can assign you someone," her boss stated, walking into her small booth she called an office in the Westchester Federal Building.

Jamika opened the folder to see a short, stocky, white man in a suit with tattoos all over his head.

"I don't do partners but who is the older man standing next to him?" Jamika asked looking at a photo of two men coming out of an Italian restaurant in Manhattan.

"Where you been hiding under a rock? That's Joe Da Don. I tried to arrest him twice and he beat both cases like Rocky, that wise ass," her boss stated.

"So, I'm taking on both of their cases?"

"No, only Sergio. The big dogs in D.C. are investigating Joe, as we speak. I bet they nail his racist ass now," her boss said walking out her area to go talk shit with other agents.

Jamika been working hard with her bureau, slaving big cases around the city making a big name for herself.

Since the killing of Stacks, she been depressed and to make shit worse, his killer was still somewhere roaming the streets.

The night she went to his car shop in Brooklyn, she was surprised to see tons of drugs and money in his safe and inside of some cars in his lot.

What she found odd that her duffle bags full of money, all had the name Web on them. When she did her research on the man name Web, she came up with nothing. It was like he was a made-up person.

Jamika also found weird how she was building a case on Murda and her case disappeared into the wind. Her boss told her to leave the case alone because what she had couldn't be used in the Federal court.

Looking at her new caseload, it was something about the two men that rubbed her the wrong way.

She placed the folder in her purse and planned to leave work early today. She needed to catch up on some sleep. She wanted to go shopping because summertime just hit after a long cold winter.

Jamika donated all of Stacks' money she found to a charity in Africa and she tossed all of the coke she found in the river. She hated her life was so boring. She was eager for some excitement.

*****

D.C. Federal Build

Carmilla was walking down the bright, shiny floor hallway in a Gucci suit followed by her boss Asad. Asad was born and raised in Syria but raised in D.C. where he became the chief of police for the FBI.

"Carmilla already knew who the man was because she got his file and record this morning."

The man's name was Fat Tone. He was a high-ranking member within the Mafia in Vegas but he was also connected heavy to the east coast families.

Last week, he was indicted on Federal charges ranging from everything to murders to kidnapping, thanks Carmilla's boss who went to Vegas to get the man.

"I'm Fat Tone," the man said in a deep voice as his collar was choking his fat oversize neck.

"How did I figure that?"

Fat Tone looked at the Spanish woman's curves and was turned on.

"You the one I speak to about this classified information I have?" he asked.

"Yes, but my eyes are up here not down there, papi," she said now sitting down with her legal pad and click pen.

"There is a woman running the Vegas drugs and casino operations. Her name is Chelsea. She is a very dangerous woman. She is not to be taken lightly," Fat Tone spoke truthfully.

"A woman running an MCM family?" Carmilla asked never hearing of such thing.

"Yes, but it's her father who is really in power. She is just his go-to girl."

"Who is her father?"

"The Don, Lavis The Don," he said as Carmilla's face went sour when she heard the biggest mob boss in the world's name. "Real name Donvito. He's very dangerous."

"Ok so whatever else do you have?"

"She's committed murders. I have detail for detail, but I also have info on a Mob boss out of New York named Joe. I used to do business with him and word is there is about to be a big war with him and some powerful men," Fat Tone said as she looked at the double mirror at Asad. She knew she just hit a homerun. Fat Tone spilled his guts out and Carmilla sent him back to Vegas on a mission.

*****

Brooklyn, NY

Tookie was standing at his brother's gravesite. He just placed fresh roses on his little brother YB's grave, something he did weekly.

Tookie loved his little brother. He knew YB was a loose cannon, but he was loyal to those loyal to him. His best friend Murda was also YB's best friend before Stacks killed him.

When Tookie came home from up north, he just wanted to take care of his daughter and get money without going back to prison.

Everything changed once YB was killed. He turned back into a criminal overnight and the demands wouldn't leave his body.

Now with a new war on the rise, Tookie knew he could be in a grave next to his brother any day and he didn't want that, but he knew what came with the life he lived. Before tears flooded his eyes, he turned to walk away.

"Excuse me sir, sir," A female voice said trying to chase him down.

Tookie turned around to see a beautiful white woman with a light tan, blonde hair, greenish grayish eyes, perfect eyebrows, thick lips for a white girl, and a Colgate white smile.

"What's up?" he said, stopping to glance at her thick curves and perky breast that were accentuated by the classy two-piece skirt and the soft silk top that she wore. The backless blouse also showed off her flat tummy.

"I don't mean to bother you, but you left this two weeks ago, "she said handing him a Prada glasses case with a pair of Prada sunglasses inside.

"Oh shit, thank you," he said as he thought he lost them in his Brooklyn condo crosstown.

"No problem. I see you come here a lot so I knew I would see you again," she said looking at him, lusting because he was her dream boy. He was dark brown, tatted up, long braids, big muscles as if he was a body builder, tall and handsome.

"Yeah, I visit my brother, but I'll walk you to your car if you don't mind."

"Sure, I'm parked near the red BMW i8. I wondered who could afford something like that but what's your name?" Gabby asked him as they walked on a downhill path.

"I'm Terell, what's your name?" he said looking at how the sunshine off her beautiful skin without make-up.

Tookie had his fair share of white girls but this one was bad and different he was turned on by her presence, which was new to him.

"I'm Gabby, a full-time nurse, single, no kids, and very strong minded. I guess that's why I can't keep a man," she laughed.

"Maybe, they just don't know what they got."

"Maybe," she replied blushing as she made it to her silver Mercedes Benz C- class Cl450 with 3% tints.

"This you?"

"Yeah, where you parked? I'll walk you there," she said because she didn't want their time to end.

"Right here," he said pointing at the BMW i8 with the roof gone.

"Oh, okay I see you," she said climbing in her Benz.

"I would love to have your number so I can call you some time," he said closing her door for her.

"I don't think your girl will like that."

"Let me ask her. Do you mind if I take this beautiful woman named Gabby's number?" he asked her, making her laugh

"Just don't let it go to waste," she said writing it or a piece of paper before pulling off.

Chapter Seven

Valhalla County Jail

Daniel just got off of work from doing a double at his job in Westchester County jail where he was a correctional officer for ten years now.

Daniel was the younger brother of Sergio, except he lived a square life unlike his brother whom he stayed away from because he was a bad person.

He had a wife and two kids at home in Sleepy Hollow, NY. Daniel knew the life his brother lived, and he kept him and his family away from it.

Today was a long day. It was 11 p.m. and he was on his sixth cup of coffee as he walked through the parking lot on his way to his Jeep Cherokee truck.

Once he made it to his truck, he tossed his vest and work bag in the trunk. When he turned around, he saw a black young C.O. standing over him

"Can I help you?" Daniel said with a fake smile looking at the dark skin man.

"No, you can't," Live said pulling out a long blade and started to stab Daniel in his neck repeatedly. Daniel let out a soft scream as Live continued to butcher him like a wild animal.

Once he saw Daniel's life leave his body, he threw the man bloody, lifeless body in the the trunk.

Gunna pulled up in Jaguar, which was stolen with a dead naked C.O. in the backseat, Live hopped in and they raced out the parking lot.

Live and Gunna killed the C.O. in the backseat so Live could wear his uniform so he wouldn't look suspicious as he waited on Daniel.

"This nigga looked like he wanted to kiss you when he leaned close to your face," Gunna laughed as he turned into a dark area next to the highway.

"Whatever nigga come on. You got the cocktail?" Live asked as he saw Gunna pull out a bottle from under his seat with a napkin sticking out.

"You love making these shits. You gotta show me one day," Gunna stated climbing out the parked Jaguar. He walked towards Live's Chevrolet Camaro SS convertible all white. "Yo, Live come on. What the fuck you doing?" Gunna looked in the Jaguar to see Live stabbing the dead body in the backseat before climbing out with his cocktail. Live lit the glass bottle filled with all types of chemicals inside as he tossed it into the car, he set it on fire.

"Had to make sure that job was done," Live said with blood all over his face and arms as he got inside the car with Gunna. As they pulled off, the Jaguar exploded.

*****

Lil Italy, NY

Web was driving through the small narrow streets passing stores and businesses. He was in a brand-new white Wraith with clear fish bait window with stars in the roof. There were two GMC SE trucks behind him, which was his security.

Today was his first day back in New York for the first time, in close to two years now. He was checking on his lawyer and he called a meeting with his business partner who was a rich Jewish man.

He wanted to open a club in Atlanta and Miami, that's why he called this meeting today.

Once he got to the block where his change was at all, hell broke loose.

Tut!

Tut!

Tut!

Tut!

Tut!

Web heard bullets hitting the car, but it was bulletproof. Web was far from dumb.

Five men hopped out a van in broad daylight, trying to take Web and his men out with machine guns.

Web hopped out with a glock with an extended clip containing thirty rounds.

Bloc!

Bloc!

Bloc!

Bloc!

Bloc!

Bloc!

BOOM!

BOOM!

BOOM!

Web's goons took two of the gunmen out while Web killed two alone. He went to the gun range every weekend with Murda to have a perfect shot.

The last gunmen took off inside of a building, running for dear life as bullets still flew past his head.

"Damn it, we gotta get out of here," Web shouted as he hopped in his Wraith seeing civilians come out of stores being nosey. Him and his crew got the fuck out of there.

*****

Woodberry Commons Mall

Gunna and his wifey Halle was in the Fendi store at one of the biggest mall outlets in New York state.

"Baby, I'm getting this," Halle said showing him a Fendi bag with a belt and scarf attached to it.

"Okay, shit you should buy the whole store."

"No, you're going to buy me the whole store, boo. Ain't that right, zaddy," Halle said hugging his neck kissing his soft lips.

"I'll think about it. Now come on, because I'm trying to hit up this Christian Louboutin and Valentino store," Gunna said walking towards the cash register.

"Oh, you too," Halle said grabbing a couple of items she wanted.

Halle was a dime piece. She was a Brooklyn ride or die type bitch. She was nineteen with a crazy body, courtesy of her Brazilian doctor. She had gone to Brazil to get her ass, breast, and lips done.

Halle was always the baddest bitch in the hood and Gunna had taken notice of her long ago. She was a freshman at Fordham University in the Bronx where she studied Criminal Justice.

Most thought she was a model or a video vixen. She was Dominican, 5'5", bronze skin complexion, hazel eyes, long dark silk hair, phat ass, big titties with piercings on her nipples and clit. She wore her baby hair like the singer Chili, deep, dimples, long eyelashes, and pretty, white teeth.

Gunna was deeply in love with Halle. She was an official chick and she knew him in and out.

"How many pairs of Louboutin's you got? Damn nigga, your closet looks like Saks Fifth. It's supposed to be the other way around and why I am carrying your damn bags?" Halle said carrying eight bags while Gunna carried ten of hers on their way to the parking lot.

"I'm carrying your bags," Gunna replied as he saw a couple of niggas look at Halle, getting each other's attention.

Gunna was used to her stopping traffic and he didn't mind as long as niggas ain't violate or get crazy at the mouth.

Once in the parking lot, Gunna placed the bags in the trunk of Halle's Audi R8 V10 that was all pink with tints. He just brought it for her four months ago.

"Such a gentlemen, that's why I love ya," she said as she climbed in the black leather seats as Gunna got in the driver seat, started the car and took off

As he pulled off Halle, started to rub his dick in his Calvin Klein sweatpants as his dick came to life.

"To crush us," she said leaning over into his side pulled out his dick and sucked it slowly, then deep throating him coming back up.

Halle sucked the head and played with the sensitive section with her tongue ring

"Oh, shit. Work that shit," she said as he sped down the highway pushing 89 mph.

Halle was using her thick lips like a pro, making all types of slurping noises as she went ham on his dick, until he shot a hot load of cum down her throat as she swallowed it all with joy.

Chapter Eight

Cucuta , Columbia

Rafael was waiting on his guest to arrive, as he looked through some newfound information about Web, while sitting in his library.

Weeks ago, Rafael got word from an old client he used to supply before he retired, saying Web was back in New York after almost two years.

Everything was going perfect until he received this news, so Rafael took it upon himself to do some investigating on Web.

After digging into Web's history, he found out Web had a son name Jamel and a daughter name Ariana.

Come to find out, his son was being watched by the Feds for murders until he disappeared around the same time Web did, so he knew something was up.

Rafael came up with a plan because there was no way he was going to sit back and let Web come to him, so he had to make the first move.

"Come inside," Rafael yelled as he heard a light knock at the door.

A young Spanish man walked in wearing a Salvatore Ferragamo suit and a Richard Miller RM26-01 watch worth $70,000 and with a pair of dark Ferragamo shades over his cold eyes.

Eddie Vaccorello was a twenty-five-year-old assassin, born and raised in Bogota, Columbia

Eddie's parents were notorious assassins the first dangerous couple assassins in the world they killed police, drug lords, and governors. When Eddie was ten years old, his parents were found in their home bed with their throats slits and private parts cut off.

His uncle trained him how to take over the family business before he got sick with an illness. As time passed, Eddie became the best assassin in Columbia but he took on job all over the world, including China, Miami, New York and Iran.

He was a handsome young man with short hair, standing six feet, chiseled, fit in shape, dark black eyes, clean face, no hair, light skin a little pale, and very stylish. He was a pretty boy.

"How can I help you today, Mr. Rafael"? Eddie asked looking at the man who was Colombian but known as a snake with venom.

"I have a big problem in the States with this man," Rafael said passing him a photo of Web coming out his large home with guards. "I also believe he has a son that's also an issue, I want dealt with, but I don't know how he looks. I'm sure you will figure that out, but how much would you charge me for the two?" Rafael asked getting straight to the point.

"Four million with half upfront in a swiss offshore account. I will contact you with the pin numbers later," he said looking at the picture of Web looking at his Bottega Veneta, liking the man's taste of fashion.

"That's a lot of money. How about three?"

"How about I charge you one million for wasting my time and leave?" he replied.

"Okay, ok how long will it take?"

"Whenever I'm done, I'll contact you. Just make sure you're paid in full or I'll make sure my next visit won't be so nice," Eddie said with a smile as he stood to leave.

Rafael hated threats. He could tell his guards to kill him right now before he even made it off his property, but he planned to take care of the young punk later. He needed him now.

*****

Las Vegas
Ace Casino

Chelsea wore a nice red Versace dress, showing a little skin as she was having dinner in a nice classy restaurant downstairs in the casino, which she closed to have private dinners with guest.

She had ten guards near the exit and her guest also had ten guards surrounding the place.

"How are things with the family?" Chelsea asked her guest, Fat Tone sitting across from her, eating pasta and garlic bread.

"Everything is good, you know same ol' shit ," he replied nervously avoiding eye contact as much as possible.

"I just wanted to have a friendly dinner with a mob boss who follows the *omerta* code we live by," Chelsea stated, eating grilled steak.

Fat Tone was silent because he had a feeling she was fishing or trying play mind games with him.

Since he been released from the Feds to get information on Chelsea and her father, he been trying to lay low until he came up with a solid plan to feed Chelsea and her dad to the Feds.

When Chelsea called him out for dinner, he couldn't refuse. It would be highly disrespectful to deny another mob boss' invite to anything. Plus, he didn't want to look suspicious.

"How's your father?" he asked changing the subject.

"Fat Tone, how was your vacation to D.C.?" Chelsea asked skipping over his question.

"Huh? Excuse me, I'm confused" he asked now sweating.

"I'm pretty sure you heard me clearly big boy. I know you was indicted by the Feds then somehow you go to D.C., and then you're back in Vegas now as if nothing happened," she said as his eyes got wide "Don't look so surprised. I just want to know what was said," she said in a sweet voice as Fat Tone looked back to his guards.

Fat Tone guards all pulled out their guns and so did Chelsea's goons but all of the guns were pointed at Fat Tone.

Nobody would dare go against the daughter of the Don. That was a death wish for one family.

Fat Tone couldn't believe what he was seeing "I-I-I said nothing, I swear."

"Have it your way," she said looking at her AP watch full of diamonds.

Fat Tone started to choke, then cough, and then he vomited all over his pasta as blood started to pour out his mouth with foam.

He started to shake as his leaned back with his eyes rolling in the back of his head.

Chelsea finished eating her steak, paying no attention as she hummed a Brittany Spears song, “Oops I did it again.”

She had the cooks poison his pasta, so she knew it was only a matter of time before he died anyway.

Once he was dead, Chelsea grabbed her steak knife and walked over to him and cut his tongue out, as the guards turned their head at that the nasty sight.

She then pulled down his pants to see a two-inch dick with soggy wrinkle balls. Chelsea sliced his balls off and placed them in his mouth full of blood and foam.

“Send his body to the Federal Build in D.C. in FedEx mail,” Chelsea said walking off.

Chapter Nine

San Fernando, Venezuela

Web made it to the backyard of his mansion in the middle of the high peak mountains.

The backyard had two large pools, a large waterfall, land, manicured grass, a view of the mountains, a gun range, dirt road leading into the mountains for dirt bikes and hiking.

Every time Web came here to see his connect, the fresh air always made him feel as if he was home in CT on his land.

The person he was waiting for was in the pool swimming fast laps a little faster than him, which made him a little jealous as he stood there in his Armani suit, which was perfect for the Venezuela weather.

There were at least thirty guards all over the compound dressed in army uniforms. The guards were all trained by the Venezuelan government and his connect had a seat within the Council of Ministers and the National Assembly.

His connect finally climbed out the pool and Web couldn't help but stare as he saw the one-piece bikini string swallow Elena's phat ass. Her ass resembled two basketballs.

"Oh, Web. I'm sorry for keeping you. Wait, have a seat I'll be right with you," Elena stated as she grabbed a cotton Gucci towel to dry her sexy body and her Dolce & Gabbana Bikini.

Elena placed a Dolce & Gabbana silk rope over her toned body covering her iron board stomach, bib boobs, big ass, and thick thighs.

"Hey Elena, how are you doing?" Web said as she embraced him with a light hug as her long curly hair was hanging to her lower back dripping wet.

Web peeked at her pretty feet and manicured pink toes as she sat down under a large tent and crossed her legs.

"I'm great. How's everything in the States?" she asked looking at him with her bright green eyes that drove most men crazy.

At thirty-eight years, she was beautiful. She stood at five foot four inches, one hundred and thirty-five pounds, thick, white complexion, 100% Latina, thick pink lips, high cheek bones, and. dirty blonde curly hair. Unlike most, her ass and breast were all although many thought she got her body done but Elena was against it she was 100% natural.

"Things are well, but I want to double my order on my next shipment," he said.

"Oh, ok sure, but are you sure you can handle it?" she inquired.

"I can handle whatever is put in front of me," he quickly replied.

"I'll make sure everything will be perfect for you and your men, Mr. Web," she said smiling, sowing her money smile.

"I want to buy a house out here, also. I love coming out here," he stated.

"I know the perfect place for sale a couple of blocks down. It's an amazing real estate. Trust me I know, I own it," she said. "I'm go get dressed. Don't go nowhere."

"Aight Web said as she stout away as her ass bounced every step.

Web met Elena last year when he came to Venezuela on vacation. He met her on a beach she was alone, unaware she had security all over the beach. He saw how beautiful she was and asked her to have a drink with him and she agreed. Normally she avoided niggas, but she liked Web's style.

Once having drinks, the two liked each other company and spend a whole week dining and wining. Elena caught on fast to see Web wasn't just a regular nigga, he was somebody big.

One night at dinner, she asked him what it was that he did, and he told her he was a boss. Elena smiled and brought him to her mansion full of goons patrolling her land and he was shocked when she told him she was a boss bitch. Since that day, Elena been his plug. The two never had sex or no type of intercourse, just a little flirting but it was strictly business.

*****

Days Later
Manhattan, NY

Murda had a long weekend since the shipment came in early and this time, it was the most he ever saw.

Murda had clients and workers all over New York from Long Island, Bronx, Albany, Naiburg, Yonkers, Buffalo, Utica, and his little brother had a large number of clients also so moving the keys was nothing. It was just getting it off the boat safely and onto the docks.

Walking into Barnes & Noble was what Murda did in his free time. He loved to read, especially urban novels from Lockdown Publications by an author name Ronnell Tules, as well as Ca$h books.

The bookstore had two levels but Murda normally stayed on the first floor with the history books, self-help books, and street lit novels.

Murda walked around the corner, reading text from Tookie. Unaware of where he was walking, he bumped into a lady making her drop her books on the floor.

"Oh, shit. I'm sorry. I wasn't paying attention," Murda stated, bending down to pick up the lady's books, which caught his attention.

The first book he saw was *Playing in the Dark* by Toni Morrison, *The Bluest Eye* by Toni Morrison, *Sister* by Toni Morrison and *The 48 Laws of Seduction* by Robert Green.

Murda read all four books recently, which was crazy to him.

"It's my fault I was in a…"the woman paused when she saw who it was. Looking into his handsome face, she became lost in his colorful eyes to match his high yellow complexion.

Murda thought he said something wrong as he looked at one of the baddest bitches he ever saw, dressed in a Coach business suit.

"Something wrong? I said I was sorry. You look like you're about to kill me or something," he laughed, handing her the books in her shaky hands.

"Sorry I have to go. Thank you. I mean sorry," Jamika said rushing off with her heart racing.

Murda watched her rush out the store as if Son the Sam was chasing her, but for some reason, there was something about the sharp dress woman in her suit and her glowing face that couldn't shake his mind.

*****

Brooklyn, NY

Tookie was leaving his brother YB's gravesite from changing the flowers. He had to go meet with Murda.

He felt the harsh wind blow his Acre Studios pants and shirt as the sun was trying to come out from the light grey skies.

"Hey stranger," a female said making him turn around clutching his pistol on his waist. He trusted no soul, not even his own.

"Oh, hi. You scared me," he said, coming face to face with Gabby.

"I see," Gabby said seeing his gun print sticking out his designer shirt.

"What are you doing here?"

"Same thing you are doing here, and for some reason, I knew you would be here today."

"Oh, yeah? You got a GPS on me?"

"No. You're not that lucky," she replied so the both laughed.

"Funny but how's everything? You look beautiful," he said looking at her white slip-on dress.

"Life is good, but why didn't you call me?"

"I was very busy. I'm sorry."

"Are you to busy to take me out to diner this weekend?" she asked him.

"I would love to this weekend."

"Good Ms. Chaws downtown. Don't meet me there, beat me there," Gabby said walking off leaving him laughing.

Chapter Ten

Downtown Brooklyn

Gunna and Live was in the most lit club in the city on the same block as the Milk River Club.

The club was jammed packed and bottle girls were running around half naked holding bottles containing sparklers to all the VIP sections.

"Yo this shit popping tonight," Live shouted over the loud Jay-Z music catering the VIP section. They were at least twenty deep inside with a group of bitches.

"Word son. Where that bottle girl at?" Brim Ave. shouted with his deep voice as he yelled for Yazzy.

"Nigga ain't that your BM?" Gunna asked Brim Ave.

"I don't know yet blood but we are waiting on the DNA test and if it is, she ain't working here no more, Skrap," Brim Ave said looking for her through the dark crowed club from his seat.

"Go to Murray nigga," Live said sitting next to Gunna who was drinking Dom P and texting, wondering why Halle wasn't hitting him back.

Gunna's rope chain was shining when the lights hit his piece on his Dior Men vast, Luclavic de Saint Sermin pants and Chanel boots. He was dripping in designer.

Mostly everybody in the club was scammers expect Gunna and his crew. He never swiped cards, he carried cash. Garbage bags of it in his trunks.

"What's on your mind, son? You look like you need a hug, boy," Live joked.

"I don't, son. Something ain't right with wifey bro. I'ma head to the crib for tonight. Y'all niggas enjoy the night and we gotta handle something in a couple of days, Live, so be ready," Gunna stated leaving the club.

"Somebody roll with him, Skrap. Make sure he's good then we in Bed-Stuy for BGB's after party," Live said drinking Henny and Remy together, getting faded.

Halle was in the shower at Gunna's condo. When she wasn't here, then she was on the college dorm studying and enjoying the college life.

She knew Gunna was out at some club with his boys, but she didn't mind because his dick was worth waiting years for.

Halle turned off the shower because she heard a door close from the living room area.

Rushing out the shower she placed a towel around her perfect wet body and a towel wrapped around her long hair.

"Papi, that's you?" she yelled wiping the fog off the bathroom mirror making sure her face was clear and good.

Halle walked out the bathroom barefooted smiling happy he chose to come home early so he could eat her delicious pussy.

When she saw the three men in suits staring at her with pistols pointed at her, she jumped back into the wall scared to death.

"W-what are you doing here?"

"Bitch shut up. Where is your boyfriend? He thinks he can kill my brother and live to tell it?" Sergio said standing in the middle of the two big bodyguards.

"I don't have a boyfriend. You have the wrong house," Halle stated as he laughed.

"Big Mark and Vasquez go get a piece of that Mexican pussy," Sergio said as his two guards both attacked Halle.

The two men threw her on the carpet and pulled her towel off, wasting no time raping her.

"Ugh please ah," she screamed crying as Big Mark rammed his fat dick in her small tight pussy that became dry. "Please stop," she cried as Vasquez fucked her on her ass. She was going crazy, unable to take the pain causing her to pass out before both men could even nut in her.

"Damn y'all spoiled the fun. Fuck her" Sergio said as he shot her in the head four times then waited for his men to get there nut off in the dead bitch.

*****

Ten Minutes Later...

Gunna walked down his hall to see his door wide open, which made him pull out his pistol as he ran in his crib ready to shoot.

What Gunna saw brought tears to his eyes. Halle laying there with holes in her head and blood everywhere as well as semen all over her private parts, sent him into a rage.

Gunna held her in his arms as he saw his goons walking in his condo.

“Get the FUCK! OUT!” Gunna yelled as they saw the dead body before leaving, feeling their homie's pain.

There was no question in his mind that the mob was behind this and he vowed to get revenge.

Gunna ran in his room grabbed some pagers and guns under his mattress and that was all he kept in his home. He had stash houses where he kept his money and drugs because he never shit where he slept at.

*****

Manhattan

Mr. Chaws downtown restaurant was packed with families, friends, and couples as people watched their food get made in front of them.

“This food is amazing. This is my first time here,” Gabby said eating clams, rice, muscles, and shrimp since she didn’t eat meat.

“I’m glad you invited me,” he said looking at how sexy she looked in a black Chanel gown with a slit and heels.

Gabby were her hair down to her back with a little make-up and a necklace with earrings from Zimmerman jewelry. Tookie rocked a black Michael Kors suit with Stacey Adams shoes.

“Tell me more about how did you get so big and what do you do for a living really?” she said giving him a look as if he better not lie.

"While I exercised all my life and I've done three prison bids. I spend most of my time lifting weights," he said as she choked on a piece of seafood

"Oh, well have you been staying out of trouble because I know we all make mistakes in life," she stated.

"I've been focusing on legit business and living my life."

"That's good. I've never met a person like you. I like your vibe and energy. I work all day, so I don't have time to enjoy my life. You know my life is boring," she stated sadly.

"You got me in it now."

"I do. While we may have different morals and values, don't get this pretty white girl look confused. I'm a different breed, trust me," she said staring at him seriously.

"My type but what if I was to tell you I also live a deadly, dangerous life. Would you still want me?" he asked.

"Yes, as long as you're 100% honest. I'ma ride with you until the wheels fall off," she stated.

"I live a dangerous life and your life could be at risk, so we could end this respectfully now and be friends or we can get the check and go separate ways," he said seeing she was trying to get serious.

"What if I tell you I like bad boy's and I'm dawn for whatever? I don't plan on going nowhere. I'm here for the long run," she said, spoken like a true Brooklyn girl.

"Okay so just understand what you're signing up for, beautiful."

"I do. Now let's get the fuck outta here and go to my place. How about Netflix and chill? Too many white people in here," she said as he stood to leave.

Chapter Eleven

Bucaramanga, Columbia

Rafael was in the passenger's seat of the SUV filled with his guards on his way to his Roman Catholic church. He grew up being taught to pray for forgiveness and to have his sins cleaned.

Rafael had been so busy teaching his son, Flaco the business, he forgot he was still a God-fearing man and very religious person devoted to his Lord.

Riding through the Colombian poverty streets seeing kids fighting over water from a well, elderly people sleeping on card boards on sidewalks, pregnant women walking around with bare feet because they couldn't afford sandals and refugee camps everywhere.

Although Rafael was cold-hearted, he still loved his country but never did nothing for them.

Once in the large church parking lot, Rafael told his men to wait outside as he always did when he came to make confessions and talk to the priest. His priest never talked back, he only listened.

Rafael walked through the double doors down the long, red carpet between the church benches lined up in rows.

Normally, every time he came, the priest would already be in the confession booth awaiting his visit.

Rafael entered the booth with two sides that was divided by a cage and stutter.

"Priest, thank you for seeing me today again, but as you know my demands are still hunting me every night. I've killed a lot of people Priest, but I regret killing the mother of my children. I can never forgive myself for that. When I caught her fucking two of my security guards, I lost it, priest. She was in my bed sucking one dick and letting the other fuck her. Excuse my language."

"Uhm," the Priest moaned forgiving him for his foul language.

"I killed all three of them, but it was my fault. I never gave her no attention. Now my daughter hates me because I made her set up a person she fell in love with and now, he is my biggest enemy. I have to get him before he gets me. To make shit worse, I'm dying. I'm old now. I remember I used to come here when I was ten years old when I killed by brother. I'm sure you remember because it was the first time you ever touched me. At first, I was scared then you told me every time we would have sex, my sins will be washed away. I believed you until I grew up and now, I know you was only being a naughty boy. I kept me being bisexual in the closet for years. I wish you could see me now. I can take dick like a porn star. You taught me well. I only wish I could be open about who I really am deep inside, but as a cartel boss, I have to put on a mask or my kids will hate me. I think my time is up, until next week," Rafael said as he heard the priest exit the other side of the booth.

Before Rafael could even exit, the door flew open. When he saw the gun pointed at him, he got nervous but when he saw the gunmen's face, he almost pissed himself.

"Get the fuck out of here, you gay bitch," Web shouted dressed in a priest outfit. He killed the priest killed an hour ago in the back.

"Web," Rafael said at a loss for words as he slowly climbed out the booth, wondering where his guards were as he saw a young man walk in the church.

"The guards are all dead," Murda said walking down the red carpet towards them.

"Good, you got the rope?"

"Yeah."

"Tie this gay ass nigga to the cross," Web said staring at the men who killed his pops.

"So, you killed my pops? I just want to know why?" Web asked as Murda pushed Rafael to the cross on top of the stage.

"He crossed me," Rafael shouted. "Please, I can pay you millions. Whatever you want," Rafael begged as Murda was tying his wrists to the cross, then his chest and ankles.

"I figured he crossed you. That's why I'm kill you on a cross, but I can't believe I was beefing with a homo," Web said as Murda looked shocked.

"Only God can judge me," Rafael said in pain, as his body was stretched out like Jesus on the cross.

"Yeah, right," Web said pouring oil gasoline on him as Murda just watched. "Pass me that lighter."

"Wait, wait, just shoot me, please."

"Nah too easy. I'll see you in hell," Web said laughing as he tossed the lit lighter on Rafael, lighting his body on fire as he was screaming.

Murda and Web watched Rafael's body burn to crisp. Web been planning this for months. He knew every Saturday, Rafael went to this church because he offered him to come years ago but Web wasn't a religious person at all. They left the church heading to their private jet.

*****

Meanwhile in Brooklyn, NY

Rafael's hitman Eddie was watching the man he believed to be Murda, closely as he was parked in a rental car across the street from a barbershop, waiting on his target to come out.

Eddie got a little info on the person he believed to be Murda, by a chick he used to fuck in Brooklyn. A black bourgeoisie named Monica, who was a dancer.

This was an easy target because the men rolled alone everywhere, which was odd to Eddie because he heard how much of a boss the kid was, but he knew bosses moved in packs for people like him.

Eddie saw the big man who was built like he used steroids hop in a real Lamborghini with rims pulling off through the afternoon Brooklyn traffic.

Seconds later, the Chevy Equinox was six cars behind the Lambo tailing him all around Brooklyn, making pit stops at every projects in Bed-Stuy.

Little did Eddie know, Murda was in Colombia and the man he was following was Tookie. Monica gave him the wrong person because she always got the two confused.

*****

Florence, Italy

Chelsea sat in her father Donvito's bedroom, as he laid in the bed while the doctor packed up his belongs in his briefcase.

The doctor was from the States, but he was living in Italy, running two hospital in the small mob town.

"Donvito, sir you just need a lot of rest and to stay out the sunlight because your skin cancer is flaring. Your prostate cancer isn't spreading yet, but please continue the diet I gave you and you should be ok. Before I forget, no smoking," the doctor said before walking out with his white, long lab coat. He passed ten guards at his room door and sixty more downstairs.

"Thanks for coming baby," Donvito said in his raspy voice as he held his daughter's hand.

Donvito was the biggest mob boss in the world. At seventy-five, he was barely alive, but he was still running the show.

His face and body were wrinkled, skinny and discolored because of his skin cancer.

"You're going to be ok," Chelsea said softly hate seeing her father like this.

"Hopefully," he said pulling out a cigar and lighter puffing on a Cuban cigar.

"Papa, you heard what the doctor said," Chelsea said watching her father blew smoke into the air.

"Fuck him. I'd rather die than listen to a fucking cocksucker worthless piece of shit tell me what to do. Pass me that bottle of gin under your feet darling," Donvito said as she did what her father asked. "We all got a day, honey. It's not about when you die but how you die. Listen, I want you to run that casino in New Jersey and kill Tommy. He was never built for this family."

"Tommy is your nephew, papa," she replied as he gave her the evil eye.

"Family isn't family nowadays. The code we used to live by when I grew up are long gone. It used to be loyalty over royalty, now it the other way around. It's a cold grimy world. You can't trust a soul. Especially family. They'll be the first one to take everything you've built," he said in Italian.

"I can understand," she said as the two talked for two hours before he took a nap and she left.

Chapter Twelve

Cart Street, BK

Gunna and Live were parked on the dark side block in a blue Volvo S60 with tints. It was ten pm and all of the businessmen on Cart St. were closed. Most of the businesses were owned by the Mafia.

Since Halle's death, Gunna felt ruthless. He couldn't even go to her funeral because it felt as if her death was his fault. He gave her family $500,000, even though he knew money couldn't bring a life back.

"You sure you want to do this?" Live asked, because he had better ideas, like to find Sergio and kill him and everything he loved.

"Yeah, this going to hit his and Joe's pockets then we go to plan b, hunting time, just in time for a cold winter," Gunna stated still confused as to how Sergio found out where he lived, because he kept his private life private.

"Aight son. We going to toss two cocktails bombs in each store. There's eight stores. You take four and I'll take four across the street. They all belonged to Joe and Sergio .I did my research," Live said, pulling his hoodie down, and placed the glass bottles filled with chemicals in two plastic bags, one for both of them.

"Let's make it fast," Gunna said as he hopped out and speed walked across the street.

Gunna took out two bottles and lit the rags on fire before throwing them into the clothing store window as fire spread through the store like a wildfire.

Live tossed two bottles in a restaurant owned by Joe, busting the windows out as the place went up in flames.

The men did a couple of more stores the same way and ran off, as cars drove past looking at the fire burning down almost every building on the block.

By the time firefighters came, Gunna and Live was long gone and half of the block was burned down to the ground as nosey civilians flooded the block.

*****

Washington, D.C.

The federal building was still in an uproar after a man's dead body was delivered last week.

The dead man was Fat Tone. When Carmilla heard this, she knew someone tried to send her a message and she had a feeling it was Chelsea.

After trying to trace where the box came from, she always came up empty. Whoever sent it, made sure there was no DNA, fibers, or traces to lead back to the killer.

Carmilla took it upon herself to look into Donvito and Chelsea's files and reports to come up with nothing.

She dug a little digger in her Federal database to find out Chelsea was married to a Federal agent name Chris in New York who was found viciously murdered.

What she found weirder was how their kids were murdered. All she could wonder was who would murder innocent children. She knew there was something more and deeper into the story. Chris also had a partner named Jamika. She knew she could hit her with some questions when she made her way to New York to investigate her. Carmilla got an important text from her cousin in Miami saying something happen to her father Rafael but she didn't care.

*****

Williamsburg, BK

Tookie was at Gabby's polished two-bedroom apartment in the nice brownstone area of Brooklyn.

"That was a good movie. Play Friday. That's one of my favorites. I'ma go take a shower. I had a long day at work," Gabby said kissing his lips as she walked to her bathroom connected to her room in a gown.

Tookie laid on her king size fluffy bed, looking through her Netflix section to find a movie.

Lately the two been spending a lot of time together. Even after opening two barbershops and selling tons of bricks, he still made time for her.

Gabby was everything a real man could want. He had been looking for her for his whole life. He sent his homies up north some pics of her and they told him she was killing Ariana Grande and Scarlett Johansson.

They spend many nights in each other bed without sex, just falling asleep in each other arms.

*****

Thirty Minutes Later...

Gabby stepped out the bathroom in a two-piece off-white bra and panties set showing her phat camel toe and thick thighs, flat stomach, nice round breast and her phat ass with a deep cuff. She was stacked for a white and natural.

"Damn," was all he could say as his dick busted out his Gucci boxers.

Gabby climbed in bed and they had foreplay while Tookie started to rub her phat clit. She got aroused and soaked as he slid off her now drenched panties.

The two were so caught up in their lust, they didn't even care her baby pitbull dog was in the corner lying on his stomach watching getting a hard on.

Gabby's legs were spread like an eagle as the head of his big black dick entered her wet, plump, shaved pussy. Her vagina was closed like a fist as he was having trouble entering her sex.

Once she loosened up, they were both grinding and humping on each other eagerly as his dick plunged in and out.

"Um, oh, ugh. I'm cumming," she said exploding. Her face twisted as her body started to shake from her hard organism.

Tookie tried to hold back but he couldn't. The had that type of pussy that would make a nigga nut in seconds.

Gabby positioned herself on her side as he eased his dick in her bare pussy that looked neat and delicious with intact lips.

"Shit, yesss," she yelled feeling his massive dick beat her walls down as she moved in a slow rhythm. Her body rocked back and forth as he filled her pussy with raw dick.

Her ass was so big, it was clapping on his thigh with every stroke.

Tookie smacked her ass as it jiggled. She bit her bottom lip, looking back grabbing the headboard taking all nine inches in her little pussy.

An hour later after several rounds of rough, hot, passionate, sweaty sex, they were done and lying down, both staring at the ceiling.

"Wow," she said as her hair and forehead were covered in sweat. She never had a sexual experience so crazy.

"You put it on a nigga," he said honestly.

"Thank you, but can I be real with you and I need you to trust me," she asked him sincerely sitting up.

"Yeah what's up."

"I know who you are," she said.

"Of course, you do. I told you everything about me."

"No, you told me what you wanted too," she said sounding a little upset as he looked a little confused.

Tookie hoped she wasn't one of them bitches that get some dick and get crazy.

"You're not being clear. Spill it," he said.

"They call you Tookie, your brother is YB, you work with two of the most dangerous men in the state, Murda and Web," she said calmly.

"Your gun is in my drawer, but I told you, you can trust me, Tookie. My brother is a man who is out for y'all blood."

"Who's your brother?"

“I’m 100% Italian and my brother is Sergio. He works for my cousin Joe, the mob boss who your people are at war with,” she said as Tookie knew he fucked up fallen for the enemy.

“Fuck, fuck, fuck, fuck. Hold on, so this whole time, you knew this so you were trying to set me up?” he asked getting pissed.

“Oh no, nothing like that. Believe me. Before we went on our first date, I went to my brother’s home to blame my other brother’s murder on him, then I saw your photo. I saw and read things about you and your crew that scared me at first, until I realized I really wanted to be with you,” she said.

“So, what about your brother?”

“Fuck that rapist. When I was a little girl, he used to rape me,” she said with tears.

“Damn, I’m sorry,” he said holding her, wondering if she could be trusted.

“I’m on your side. I will never cross you, baby,” she said looking into his eyes as they both made love for another two hours. This time more passionately.

Chapter Thirteen

Wall Street, NY

Mueller just got off of work leaving his stock agency he owned. He pulled a double tonight because the numbers on Wall St. been below average all day.

Mueller was an Italian man with a beautiful wife who lived in Rockland County in their big mansion.

He was waiting for a cab so he could take the train home as he did every day instead of driving his Benz in the crazy New York traffic going and coming from work.

Life wasn't all peaches and cream for the rich man. He grew up in Brooklyn around the mafia. He chose to go to college and start his own stock company instead of becoming a mobster like his brother Joe did.

Joe and Mueller had a strong disliking for each other. They both thought they were destroying their family legacy.

Finally, able to wave down a cab, Mueller climbed in the yellow cab in his Canclini suit and briefcase looking like a true businessman.

"Union Square please," Mueller told the African driver as the cab pulled off into the city traffic.

It was dark outside tonight. Mueller hated working overnight even though he was having an affair with his new young assistant.

The cab was speeding through traffic almost running red lights, which made Mueller put his seatbelt on.

"You mind slowing down sir?" he yelled from the backseat as he looked out the window to see the driver was going the opposite way from Union Square train station. "You're lost?" Mueller questioned, as he saw the driver was pulling up into a dark alley.

"Huh?" The cab driver smirked as the light hit his face for the first time.

Muller saw how young the driver was and the crazy look in his eyes and instantly became nervous.

"I think I'ma walk," Mueller said taking off his seatbelt and trying to open the door as the cab parked next to a Nissan Rogue truck.

"Not so fast son," Live said turning around with a gun pointing at Mueller's head.

"Please, I don't have nothing to do with Joe's business. Please, I got a family."

Boom!

Boom!

Boom!

Boom!

Boom!

Live blew his brains out on the cab backseat window. Live hopped out leaving Mueller's dead body in the backseat as he walked towards the trunk, popped it and came face to face with an Indian man that was tied up.

"Sorry, kid you should've chose a different field," said Live as he shot the driver in the head one time before he got inside the Nissan pulling off out the alley.

*****

Downtown Brooklyn

Jamika was inside of her favorite coffee shop. She went to every morning before she went to work in White Plains.

Once he ordered her coffee, she grabbed her USA Today newspaper, took a seat in the back of the shop at her favorite seat, and turned to the *World* section.

She had been so busy working on the Sergio case, she had been clueless to what was going on in the worldly news. The first article was a story of a drug cartel boss found burned to death on a cross.

"Damn," she remarked, as an image of Rafael burned on a cross formed in her mind.

Last week, Sergio and his boss' businesses were burnt down. Jamika found that shocking. She knew it was a big war in the city right under her nose, but she was lost as to with who.

As she was reading the newspaper, she saw a shadow standing over her, which made her look up.

"Excuse me, do you mind if I speak to you for a second, Ms. Jamika?" Murda said seeing the surprised look on her face.

Jamika was confused as to how he knew her name. She looked at his black expensive suit and GMT Master Rolex watch and nodded her head.

"What do you want?" she said coldly, as she acted as if she was still reading her newspaper.

I want to know why an agent such as yourself, made me her number one target?" Murda asked.

"Sorry but you're far from number one and if you didn't disappear, then I would have your pretty boy ass right in Pollock USP somewhere doing life," she said with a fake smile looking into his beautiful eyes.

"I would love have the most beautiful woman I've ever seen, place me in cuffs any day."

"Your wish is my command. Now what else do you fucking want?" she replied.

"I just wanted to introduce myself. It's only right but have a good..." Murda was cut off as an older black couple approached them.

"Excuse us young people, but me and my husband been together fifty years and when we saw you two, we thought about ourselves years ago. You two look perfect together. May God bless the both of you," the older light skin woman said with her husband behind her.

"Miss, we're not..." Jamika stated before Murda cut her off.

"We aren't anything except for two young people trying to find love. This is the woman I plan to spend the rest of my life with," Murda said.

"Aww so cute. You two take care." The old lady walked off smiling with her husband as Jamika rolled her hazel eyes at Murda.

"Good luck," Murda stated as he stood to leave.

Jamika was pissed but her panties were soaking wet and sticking to her pussy. She had to stay strong. There was no doubt Murda was the sexist man she ever saw but he was a killer and she knew this.

She saw him pull off in a white Bugatti Chiron worth four million dollars,

She was ready to leave. She was going to nail Murda's ass once and for all. She just needed to find hardcore evidence on him.

Once outside, she saw something on the windshield of her Lexus. When she got closer, she saw a Toni Morrison's book *Beloved* with a dozen pink flowers, which made her smile.

Jamika looked around to make sure nobody saw her blushing as she placed the items in her car before climbing inside.

She couldn't lie to herself, if he wasn't a criminal, she might've gave him a taste of her good pussy.

*****

West Philly, PA

Kristie was Joe's ex-wife. She was an ex-model in her early fifties who was still tall and beautiful, with minimal wrinkles and bags under her eyes.

She moved to Philly ten years ago after divorcing Joe. She was now a nurse at an elder home in West Philly.

Kristie had two grown kids, who lived in Utah and were happily married with kids. Her and Joe still messed around daily. He was still in love with her.

He was the reason for divorce because he was a cheater and lived a deadly lifestyle.

Her doorbell rang as she was cooking dinner for herself.

"Who's there?" she said walking to the door in her sunflower dress.

"Gabby."

"Oh my God, Gabby, "Kristie said rushed to open her door for her. Kristie hadn't saw her in five years since she came to see her in Philly.

When she opened the door, Gabby looked beautiful in her Gucci mini skirt and cropped top. Gabby grew up around Kristie babysitting her. They were all close family and she knew how much Joe loved her.

"How you been?" Gabby asked.

"Great! You're just in time for dinner. I'm sure we have a lot to catch up on," Kristie said turning around to see Gabby pointing a gun at her.

"I'm sorry." Gabby shot her six times in the heart as her body hit her old carpet as she blead to death.

Gabby ran out the house as Tookie was parked outside the quite neighborhood.

"I did it, babe," Gabby said excited, loving the power she felt holding on to a gun.

"Good job. Let's go home," Tookie stated as he thought checkmate to himself pulling off.

Chapter Fourteen

Milan, Italy

It was fashion week in Milan and Web was front row seat at the Fendi show, watching models sport the newest Fendi gear up and down the runway.

Web was dripped in Fendi as well as his sixteen-man crew surrounded him.

Fashion week was big for the biggest mob bosses and drug lords around the world. Web was watching the women strut up and down the runway, while sipping a glass of expensive Moet.

He saw a lot of Mob bosses in the room. There were some he knew and some he didn't, but he was only here to enjoy himself.

Carmilla just entered fashion week at the Fendi show. She wore a beautiful Ferdi slit tight dress with her hair in a bun, looking beautiful shutting down there bold as everybody stared at her.

She was here tonight because she heard Donvito was supposed to be present tonight at fashion week as he was every year.

Carmilla was seated in the middle of the large crowd, fill of fashion freaks and news reporters.

The show was going well, but she didn't see Donvito or his goons at all, which was odd because Fat Tone swore he came every year.

Carmilla saw a handsome light skin man sitting in the front surrounded by big football players as if he was a famous rapper.

When the man turned his head, Carmilla got a better look at him and she was at a loss of words as her heart started to race.

Web was really enjoying the show. He had a couple of clothes items he wanted to get from the show tonight.

Something told him to look to his far left following the crowd's eyes. He saw a sexy white woman with long red hair walk through the doors in a dark gray dress with a grey mink over her shoulders.

Web saw over twenty something guards with her protecting her. He knew the woman was somebody whoever she was from.

The woman was walking towards him as Web continued to watch the show until the woman and her men stepped in front of him.

"Web, good to see you," Chelsea stated standing in front of him smiling.

Web was at a loss for word he had no clue it was Chelsea looking so good. He heard she moved to Miami after his nieces and brother was murder.

"Chelsea, good to see you. I see a lot has changed," Web said looking at her goons.

"Yes, a lot has, but I am going to my seat. Take care and stay out of trouble," Chelsea said with a chuckle, walking off like a diva.

Web couldn't believe what he was seeing he knew she had to have been fucking someone with power or she hit a lotto.

Whatever it was, Web was going to make sure he found out because something was off with Chelsea's vibe.

*****

Downtown Brooklyn

"I want all of these niggers dead before the end of the month or there is no deal," Joe shouted in front of his guest.

"First of all, watch your fucking mouth when you use the word nigger around me, and second, you don't put no fucking time period on my work. Do I make myself clear, cracker?" Big Dave stated sternly, looking into Joe's eyes showing no fear, standing up for his black race.

"Okay just let me know when the jobs are done," Joe told Big Dave as he stood to leave.

Big Dave was a hitman, born and raised in Yonkers, NY, but he did a lot of big hits for the mob in his twenty-five years of the killing business. He was a professional hitman. He left scenes without a trace and never spending a day in jail.

When Big Dave left his pawn shop, he made a few calls. Since all of his businesses were burned down, he been mad at the world because he only had two businesses in New York.

The insurance company was going to pay him for all his losses but those businesses had been a part of his family for years.

Sergio wasn't doing a good enough job at dealing with Web's goons. He had pictures of all of them and he vowed to bury all of them.

*****

Days Later

Murda was coming out his Pink House projects after winning $150,000 in a dice game in the park. It was midnight and Murda was about to head home to his condo in the Bronx Uptown.

He still came through. He did to show love. Not to mention, he was supplying the whole East New York so everybody loved him.

Murda wasn't with the idea of riding around with security all day. He was a hood nigga who love to boot his gun.

Focused on Jamika lately, he had been tailing her moves here and there to see if she was on his line again, but she wasn't. It seemed as if she was on something bigger because she was spending a lot of time in her Italian areas.

Once he made it to his Bugatti, he felt a gun pressed against his curly hair.

"Would you like to face your killer?" the man asked with a deep voice.

"Facto," Murda said turning around with his hand up to see a big black ugly motherfucker who looked like the nigga from *Green Mile* with no facial hair or eyebrows, just a killer look.

"May Allah forgive your sins."

Bloc!

Bloc!

Bloc!

Bloc!

Bloc!

Bloc!

Murda thought his life was over until the man's body fell on him. His body was filled with holes as he saw Gunna with a smoking gun. Gunna was following the men since he left Joe's office knowing he was trouble.

"Let's get out of here," Murda said to Gunna as they climbed in the foreign car and raced out the lot.

Chapter Fifteen

Bogota, Colombia

Rafael's son, Flaco was in his ranch style summer house in the woods just of an old country road.

Oh, ugh…" the skinny pretty Spanish woman wailed as Flaco's dick was ramming in her swollen pussy from behind. She was eating the other woman's pussy who was flat on her back with her legs in the air.

"Aaahhh shh. I'm cumming-g-g," the Spanish woman yelled. She squirted all over her girlfriend's face.

Flaco saw the other woman squirt, which made him go harder as he placed a thumb in her ass. She began groaning and moaning.

"You got some good pussy" Flaco shouted as she tightened her inner walls as he jerked his hips forward as her body bounced forward with every thrust as he released his warm thick semen inside of her.

"Fuck me, now," the other said, feeling a little jealous her girlfriend was getting all the dick.

This wasn't Flaco's first threesome with Jessica and Isabel. They were two bad ass Spanish bitches who was down for whatever.

When he pulled out of Isabel, her and Jessica both started to suck his average size dick taking turns.

Jessica wrapped her thick lips, she recently had plastic surgery on, and slid her head up and down his shift covering his dick in spit mixed with precum as she took inch by inch.

Isabel tickled his balls with the tip of her tongue then sucked his balls as Jessica forced his dick down her throat.

"Mmmmm," Flaco moaned looking at both women, admiring their skills.

Isabel took his dick into her wet, warm mouth and started to increase the speed giving him first sloppy as she soaked the sheet with his nut.

"Uhm," both women moaned sharing his cum. They were kissing each other as Flaco watched with a hard dick because he was on strong, powerful ecstasy.

Jessica climbed on his dick, sitting on it as her thick hips rolled slowly grinding at his dick as Isabel sat on Flaco's face as he ate her pussy, parting her thin lips and sucking her mushroom clit.

"Oh my God. Oh, oh, sss," Jessica yelled as she was banging on his hard dick. He grabbed her wide waist and held it in place as he pounded her pussy out as she bounced up and down, side to side like basketball.

Isabel was shaking as she was climaxing back to back. She let out deep muffles and screams as cum flowed out her small pussy. Flaco then spread her ass cheeks apart and spit in her anus then he started to eat her ass.

Jessica got in reverse cowgirl as she came on his dick.

"Oh fuck, baby," Jessica said in Spanish as Flaco pushed her off his dick because her pussy was loose, and he couldn't get a nut.

Flaco grabbed Isabel's petite frame and bent her over as he tore her ass up and placed her head on the pillow. The sexual threesome was hot and heavy.

"Fuck my ass, papi," Isabel said so Flaco smeared his wet tongue over her ass hole then slowly entered her tight anus. "Oh, no. Sss, oh fuckkk," she screamed as Jessica spread her ass cheeks as Flaco forced his dick into her tight small ass.

"Back that ass up. Take it," he said grabbing her grail shoulders, ramming her back into his dick as her small ass dance on his upper thighs.

"Ugh…no, too much," she yelled feeling his dick tear her core.

Flaco grabbed her long hair and yanked her back as she took all of his dick. He started to punch her ass out as she went crazy biting and pulling on the pillows, ripping the cotton out because it was too painful for her. Once she felt him nut in her ass, she pushed it out making it drip into her pussy.

The women wanted more but Flaco had a meeting in less than an hour.

"Get the fuck out," Flaco told both women as he started to get dressed. "Go pleasure my men," he told both women, who looked at each other knowing it was going to be a long day. Last time they fucked ten niggas at once, their bodies were sore for two weeks. They were only nineteen years old. The guards always loosened their pussy.

Flaco laughed when he saw Isabel's skinny ass limp out with his cum all over her ass and pussy.

Flaco went in his walk-in closed fill of designer clothes, shoes, belts, coats, underclothes and hats. He went into his jewelry box and put on a diamond ring his father gave him worth two point three million dollars and a bracelet.

Since Flaco's father was murdered, he took over the legacy. Rafael was preparing him for this day for years and at twenty-three years old, he was advanced and on top of his game. He had all of his pop's clients and plus his own so he was already seeing millions. Before his father died, he told him about a man named Web that was out for his life and if anything was to happen to him, Web was responsible.

Flaco planned to take care of the man Web when the time came. He was focused on business and getting richer.

*****

White Plains, NY

Jamika was at work reading a police report of Sergio's brother and how he was stabbed to death, then blocks away another man was found killed and burned to death.

She also saw how someone burned down his businesses and killed Joe's brother who was a rich stockbroker.

Jamika thought about the case where a young girl was raped and killed named Halle in an apartment, but what caught her attention was when the neighbor said in a police report, she saw three Italian men enter and leave before she was killed.

It wasn't hard to put two and two together. Halle had to know someone who was having issues with the Italians. She called the neighbor on her cell phone to ask her if the girl had a boyfriend or brother that was any danger and had any known enemy.

After spending five minutes on the phone, she had a name of the girl's boyfriend. His name was Gunna. The woman told her he was a very respectful kind kid and she believed his family was rich because he had a lot of luxury cars and jewelry, but Jamika knew better.

She typed the kid's name up to see he was a basketball player, his mom was recently murdered in Cypress two years ago, and he had a brother name Jamel. When she saw the name, her heart stopped.

"Can't be," she said as a knock scared her. She logged off her computer to see a beautiful Spanish woman walked in in a nice grey blazer from Gucci.

"Hey, are you Jamika?" asked Carmilla.

"Yes, hi. You must be Carmilla from D.C." Jamika said standing to shake her hand. D.C. was the Federal headquarters so anyone from D.C. was in high power and called all the shots.

"Can I sit?"

"Sure, please."

"I hope I'm not interrupting you, but I just want to connect these with Joe and Sergio then bring them down," Carmilla stated.

"I'm glad to have you," she replied pulling out a file with photos of Joe and Sergio.

"Two heads are better than one, but do you have anything good?" Carmilla said pulling out her own folder.

"Check these out. This is a photo of Sergio and Joe at a funeral in Philly. I believe it was his ex-wife. This is a photo of him and Sergio at Joe's daughter funeral, then I have photos of them at each other brother's funeral. All are recent," Jamika said.

"Whoever they are at war with, are up by one hundred but they are not leaving any clues, DNA, or witnesses."

"Do you think it could be another Mob family or a Cartel family? Those are the only people I can think of capable of this type of shit," Jamika said as the hard rain hit the build window.

"I don't really know yet but speaking of Mob families, have you ever heard of this woman?" Carmilla said passing her a photo of Chelsea.

"Oh, my fucking God. Yes, Chelsea is my ex-partner wife before he was murdered," Jamika said sadly looking at the picture of Chelsea.

"She is the daughter of the biggest Mob boss in the world. Do you think Chris had any ties to the Mob as far as anything that could get him killed?" Carmilla said.

"Before he was killed, he was asking me for money. A lot of money and nervous as if he owed…oh shit it make sense. His kids was killed and him because he owed money to the MOB," Jamika said, mad she hadn't figured this out before.

"Now we have to figure out what part she has in all of this. After we figure these two out," Carmilla stated looking at pictures of Joe and Sergio.

Chapter Sixteen

Brooklyn

Tookie and Gabby were holding hands as they were walking out of the movie theater into the parking. The dark skies gave the parking lot a pitch-black look because the parking lot lights were out.

"Babe how was the movie?" Gabby asked clutching his big, muscular arm.

"That was a real white people movie."

"It was a love story. You sound so racist."

"That shit was whack. We should of went to see that Black Panther movie like I said," Tookie replied feeling the night breeze in his Balmain sweater as Gabby wore a Balmain dress to match his fly.

"Now how would that look me being the only white girl in there with blond hair and blue eyes? Trying to get me killed already," she said as he started to laugh hard.

Gabby recently moved in with Tookie after he begged her to. She was the perfect woman. She cooked, cleaned, was loyal, sexy, independent and smart.

Beef with the Italians been crazy, but Tookie had an upper hand. Gabby she informed him everything he needed to know about Sergio and Joe. Tookie told her to lay low with her social media accounts and their love life at best until shit died down.

As they made it to the Ferrari 488 GTB coupe Tookie recently brought, shots fired off as they both went into action.

Gabby spun around and grabbed a pistol from her thigh hostler and started shooting at the single gunman. Gabby had her gun license and she was a great shooter, something nobody knew about her.

Tookie was ducked down shooting back and forth with the young Spanish man across the lot as the shots went back and forth.

Eddie was waiting two hours for the two to come out so he could head back to his hotel to prepare for Web next, but little did he know Rafael was dead, so his other two million dollars was dead with him.

"Damn it," Eddie yelled hiding behind a van as the white girl and big muscle head nigga wasn't backing down. He saw a cop car enter the parking lot.

Not trying to go to prison, Eddie dashed across the lot shooting at the couple but he caught two shots to his side as it burned.

"Fuck!" Eddie yelled as he climbed in his rental, racing the opposite of the cop car at the lot.

Gabby saw she caught him twice in his side as she saw red and blue lights.

"Cops," Tookie stated as the cop car was now in front of them.

"Freeze! Now drop the gun," a white young officer shouted ten feet away from them, hiding behind his driver door panel.

Gabby faked as if she was going to drop her gun and shot the officer twice in his neck. He tried to call it in, but his body collapsed into a slow death. Tookie looked at her as if she was crazy and fired four shots at the officer's head killing him.

"Get in the car," Tookie yelled as he hopped in the driver's seat as she got in the passenger's seat.

The Ferrari burnt rubber through the back entrance as cops flooded the main exit, but they were long gone turning onto the exit on the highway around the corner from the movie theatre.

"I guess dinner is over with for tonight. Wendy's drive thru sounds like a plan," Gabby said showing her perfect smile.

Tookie looked at the bitch as if she was insane. He now knew for a fact Gabby was a different type. He had no clue she had a gun or was an amazing shooter. She saved his life.

"You saw his face."

"Yeah, Spanish, Colombian, or Brazilian."

"Good I got a plan," Tookie said smiling.

*****

Co-op City, Bronx

"Thanks for taking me out, Live. Since you came home, a bitch don't even see you no more, my nigga like damn," Victoria said as she ate outside in the back of the seafood restaurant.

"You know how shit be when a nigga trying to chase a bag. I don't even have time for myself or mama, luv," Live replied taking a sip of his Pepsi soda watching a couple of Bronx niggas stare at his two gold necklaces hanging from his neck, wishing they would try anything.

"There's a lot of talk about you and Gunna in the hood. When you going to change your life?" Victoria asked seriously.

Victoria was a pretty brown skin chick that was thick in all the right places, brown chinky eyes because she was half Korean. Her mom was from Pyongyang, North Korea.

She was in college at NYU. She was smart, majoring in art graphic design. Tookie was her first. Even when he went off to jail, she still wrote him, pictures, visits and kept a friendship even though she moved on because she wasn't doing jail time with no nigga that she wasn't married to.

"Don't believe everything you hear, but how's school? He asked changing the subject

"I'm on fall break now, but its good. I'm focused. I saw your mom and pops going to Jummah the other day," she said as she checked her G-shock watch. She seen it was 11 p.m. and her curfew was midnight because her parents were strict on her and all her sisters.

"That's good. I ain't stop by in weeks," Live said sounding sad about it.

Live's parents banned him from coming back into their home until he got on the straight path. Allah provided for him. They knew what he was into. Half of Brooklyn did. He was a little King Tut.

"You should soon, but I have to go home."

"You want your birthday present?"

"Oh you ain't forgot?" she said smiling.

"Never here you go," Live said handing her a set of BMW keys belonging to the white BMW X4 parked out in the parking lot.

"No, you didn't. Oh my God, Live. I can't."

"Yes you can. Please you gave me loyalty and support for three years. It's no price tag on that, but this is the least I can do. Now come on, drive me to the hood," Live said sitting to leave as she followed.

As soon as they stepped foot into the parking lot, it was all-out war!

Boc.

Boc.

Boc.

Boc.

Boc.

Boc.

Boc.

Boc.

They were ambushed as well as four other civilians. Live pulled out and grabbed Victoria while shooting at the five gunmen running down on him.

BOOM.

BOOM.

BOOM.

BOOM.

BOOM.

Live took two of the masked men out as he took over near an outside table.\

"Victoria you ok?" Live said looking down for the first time to see she was shot three times in her chest, coughing out blood. "Nooo!! Hold on," Live yelled with tears as he stood up continuing to shoot.

Boc.

Boc.

Boc.

BOOM.

BOOM.

BOOM.

Two Bronx niggas popped up from nowhere, shooting at the gunmen killing one while the other two ran off but one picked up Live's wallet.

When Live looked at Victoria, she was gone, lying in a puddle of blood. Twenty feet next to him was a fourteen-year-old girl dead as her brother from the Bronx cradled her crying and screaming.

Live had to get out of there he kissed Victoria on her thick glossy lips and run off to the BMW.

Chapter Seventeen

Queens, NY

Carmilla was walking into her condo lobby to see two guards there patrolling the lobby as they always did.

"Good evening gentlemen," Carmilla said walking passed both men who eye fucked her. It was something she was used to.

Carmilla got in the elevator. She was drained. Her and Jamika was spending a lot of time working on the big case, but something told her Jamika was holding something back.

Once on the fifth floor, she entered her apartment she had for years that nobody knew about.

Her condo was large, next to a park, so the view was beautiful, Versace furnishing throughout the crib, a fireplace, antique design wallpaper, stainless steel kitchen, zebra marble tile, three bathrooms and four bedrooms.

This was her get away when she wanted to get away from work and issues.

Carmilla turned on her crib light and took off her blazer hanging it on the wall hangers near the doorway hall.

She was ready to unwind as she walked into her kitchen and grabbed a bottle of strong wine, and made her way to the living room to watch the Oxygen channel.

"What the fuck," Carmilla shouted pulling out her Glock 17 from her hip pointing it at the man who sneaked in her condo.

"So now you're going to kill me? Go ahead, this won't be the first time you crossed me," Web said in his soft voice, sitting on her single couch wearing a Marc Jacob suit with a Rolex, diamond rings and an icy bracelet.

"Web what the fuck are you doing here?" she said with mix feelings still aiming the gun at him.

"No beautiful, the question is what are you doing here?" he replied.

"I should kill you right her for how you did me. You kept me as a fucking slave," she shouted, remembering how she was tied up in a basement two years ago.

"I had to, Carmilla. You tried to ruin me and everything I built, and I fell for your fake love," he said now standing up, walking to her living room window that had a view of a nice park.

"I was honest with you Web."

"After I found out you was the FBI. Did you get a bonus for marrying me?" Web said laughing

"No, I didn't, but I wish I did. Was you going to kill me? That question played in my mind since you disappeared," she asked still aiming her gun at the only man she ever loved.

"To be honest Carmilla, I wasn't. I just needed to figure some shit out so, me leaving town was all I could do."

"You didn't have to do that because someone above my office made your case disappear. You must have powerful connections or just lucky," she said dropping her gun.

"I didn't know that," Web said honestly, wondering who dropped his case or the investigating.

"I tried to cover you, Web, but don't even know."

"I saw you at Milan Fashion week. You looked beautiful in your Fendi dress," Web said as looked shocked she had no clue he saw her.

"Why are you here Web? How did you know where I lived?"

"That should be your least worry, but I'm very concerned as to why you're in town working with the other young woman."

"I'm in town on work and it's none of your business."

"I believe it is Carmilla. Do you know your still my wife?" Web said looking at their wedding ring on her finger and she saw his, which made her heart melt, but she kept a poker face.

"I see you finally paid my father a visit," she said staring at him knowing he is the one who killed her father Rafael.

"I don't know what you're talking about, but I believe in karma. You should too," he said.

"That's my middle name, but you can get the fuck at my house and if you come back, I'll be sure to kill you, papi," she said smiling.

"Okay, I hope to see you around," he said walking towards her.

Carmilla was wet at the sight of him. He still looked the same, just a little stockier and his Tom Farrell perfume turned her on more.

"Before you leave, you wouldn't have nothing to do with this mayhem with the Mafia, would you?" she asked as he stepped at her door.

"Carmilla, I am boss. You still a pig. It's a thick line between us and you're a smart woman," he said reaching for the door.

"Web be safe," she said before he walked out. When the door closed, Carmilla fell on her floor crying for so many reasons. She just cried for them all. He did something to her soul. Her life was empty without him and she saw it in his eyes also.

*****

A.C., New Jersey

Lil Tommy was in the casino office watching his laptop screen with his feet up on the desk. He was enjoying his porno he was watching.

"Ummmm," he gritted, watching a black student bang an older white woman dressed up like a teacher.

Lil Tommy was far from little. He was short five foot four, weighing 385 pounds and walked with a wobble.

He was born and raised in Jersey City, with his Mafia family who ran New Jersey under Donvito's ruling.

Lil Tommy managed one of Donvito's casinos only because he was his nephew, but he wasn't the killer type like most of his family. He just loved to sniff dope and fuck hookers on the daily.

"Come on, choke her," Lil Tommy said slowly stroking his little meat as his office door flew open and Chelsea streamed in with her goons.

"Chelsea, do your clients know how to knock!" Lil Tommy yelled almost falling out his chair trying to put his underwear on and slacks.

Chelsea heard the loud porn on his computer and her men were laughing

"I see you're still a freak, little guy," Chelsea said as she wore a pink Chanel dress with pink pumps showing her manicured pink toes.

"Chelsea, what are you doing here? I thought you were in fucking Vegas," he said closing his computer.

"You thought wrong, fat boy, but I like what you've done with the casino. More slot machines, more bars, new carpet, more employees, good work," she said sitting down crossing her sexy toned legs as Lil Tommy tried his hardest trying to look under her skirt. He had a feeling she had a hairy, bushy pussy as he liked it. He didn't really care if they were first cousins or not.

"You here to visit?"

"No, you fucking prick! I'm taking over," she stated, pulling out a 9mm gun and shooting him in his forehead. "Clean this office. I know there's semen all over the place," she said disgusted, walking out to go have a drink.

Chapter Eighteen

Long Island, NY

Eddie was lying in the hospital bed still in pain from being shot by Gabby. He had to admit she was a mean shooter, but he couldn't wait to be released so he could kill the both of them.

Eddie still thought Tookie was Murda. He had no clue where the man Web was. This was Eddie's hardest job by far. If he would of knew this task would be this difficult, he would have charged Rafael triple.

He planned to give Rafael a call once he was released from the hospital in a day or two, still unaware of this death.

After being shot two nights ago, he knew he couldn't go to a hospital in Brooklyn or that would of draw red flags, so he went to the closet hospital, almost dying as he passed out in the lobby.

The nurses gave him heavy pain meds after being shot in the kidney and lungs. He was lucky to be alive.

Using a fake ID, name, and address, he was able to tell the doctors and human resources workers to bill him for their service.

Eddie heard the door open. He knew it was time for his dinner and meds. He turned off the TV. He was sick of watching the *Family Guy* show all day even though it made him laugh, he was in too much pain.

"You ready for your meds?" a nurse said as she placed the tray in front of him on a small table.

"Thanks," he said as the nurse must have just started working because he never saw her before. She wore glasses, a mask, and a blue scrub uniform. All you could see was her eyes and long hair in a ponytail, and of course her curves.

"You're just starting?" he asked her as she was refilling his IV's.

"Yes."

"You're beautiful. Why cover your face like that?" He asked her as she walked around the bed and laughed as he looked at her nice thick ass.

"There are a lot of germs and nasty people in this world and you're one of them," the nurse said pulling out a Germany rugger pistol with a silencer attached to it from her lower back.

Eddie knew something was off about the woman. He felt a funny vibe from her.

Gabby pulled off her face mask.

"You fucking bitch. You shot me" Eddie said.

"Yeah I know, handsome but sorry, I can't stay to chat," Gabby said before shooting him nine times in his face and upper torso.

Gabby walked out the room and down the hall waving at some of her co-workers.

This was the hospital Gabby worked at as a nurse. When Eddie got shot, her and Tookie knew he needed medical attention and they knew going to a Brooklyn hospital was out the question.

Gabby called a couple of hospitals asking if a young Spanish man in his mid-twenties arrived recently and convinced he was her son and they all fell for it. Out of all four hospitals she called, Eddie was at the one she worked at, which made their plan to easy.

"Everything is ok," Tookie said sitting in a Cadillac XT5 truck in the hospital parking lot as Gabby climbed in the passenger seat.

"Yeah. The job done, daddy," she said in her white girl voice. "I even gave them my two-week notice, informing them I quit. I was sick of that job anyway.

"Good, I am taking you back to the hotel then. I'm going to holler at my man before we skip town for a while," Tookie stated.

"Okay," she said playing with her nails. The two came up with the idea to skip town until the manhunt of the police killing died down because it was on the news every hour, but the police had nothing because the movie theater cameras were down that day due to blown fuses.

*****

Parkchester, Bronx

It was eleven at night and Murda called a meeting with Gunna and Tookie, after speaking with his father last night.

Shit was getting real. He'd come close to losing his life last week if it wasn't for Gunna saving his ass and he still hadn't had the chance to thank him. Murda knew he was sleeping on his little brother, but him and Live were bringing pain to the Mob.

Murda was living in the Bronx, but he also had a couple of more spots in Mount Vernon and Staten Island to rest his head away from Brooklyn. Gunna also brought a condo Uptown in the Bronx after Halle got killed in his crib in Brooklyn.

Walking into the parking lot in the back of the complex, he saw a shadow leaning on his Bugatti, but he could tell it was a female because of the long hair.

"You lost? That's my car," Murda shouted getting closer to the woman. He then noticed it was the Federal cop bitch, Jamika. He couldn't lie to himself. She was looking like a snack in her black Celine strapless dress with Christian Louboutin's on her feet showing her pretty toes

"Going out clubbing?" she asked looking at his Balenciaga shirt, rope necklace, American Apparel jeans, Giuseppe shoes and a Patek Philippe yellow gold watch. "No, I'm not lost at all, Murda," she said looking into his bright colorful eyes and curly good hair.

"What can I help you with and you're leaning on a four-million-dollar car."

"I don't give two fucks about your car or dirty money. I want to know what do you and your little brother Gunna having going on with Joe, Sergio and the mafia," she said sternly seeing his facial expression turn into a frown.

"Your digging yourself in something you may not get out of."

"Don't you dare threaten me."

"I didn't, it's a promise."

"The mafia is having a big case against them and you and your crew is right on the middle. I'm trying to fucking help you," she said, getting frustrated.

"You can help me by getting out my way. I have somewhere to go," he said as she slowly moved. He climbed in his luxury car smelling her Hermes perfume

"Fine, I warned you okay. I'll go to your funeral. You're just like this rest of them," Jamika stated as Murda hopped out his car and got in her face.

"You don't know shit about me or my life or why I risk my life to take care of my people. I can never be like the rest because I'm doing what most will never do, so next time you judge, know me first," he said face to face with her looking into her hazel eyes.

Jamika was shocked he just went in on her. She was at a loss for words.

Jamika rushed in and kissed his lips as he kissed her back passionately for at least ten seconds.

"Oh my God. I can't. What I'm doing?" she said out loud as she rushed off. Murda grabbed her arm but she pulled away and ran to her Lexus

When he saw her race out the lot, he got in his car heading to Brooklyn. All he could think about was her.

*****

Brooklyn

Murda pulled up under the Brooklyn Bridge to see a Cadillac and a Maserati parked side by side as Tookie and Gunna were talking on the waterfront walkway.

"We got a big issue. The Feds are on Joe and Sergio so there close to us," Murda said as soon as he approached them.

"Fuck, so what do we do now?" Gunna asked.

"We gotta kill them because if we don't, they are going get knocked and rat on us anyway and I'm not trying to go to jail if I can prevent it," Murda said.

"Facts but I got a little issue myself. I met a chick. Come to find out, she's is Sergio's sister."

"Did you kill her?" Gunna asked him.

"Of course, he did," Murda stated speaking for him.

"Not really."

"What the fuck you mean?"

"What the fuck it sound like? She's been helping me put this work. She killed Joe's ex-wife and a nigga someone sent at us. Plus, she killed a cop for me," he stated as they looked shocked.

"A nigga tried to kill you?" Murda asked.

"Yeah a Spanish nigga, son. He looked foreign."

"Oh, shit that must have been Rafael's people. He's dead.

"Yeah she killed him, but we on the move from killing that cop at the movies."

"Damn, that was you? That shit all over TV," Gunna said.

Murda didn't respond other than a slight chuckle. The men talked some more then went their way.

Chapter Nineteen

East New York, BK

Live's parents were both in the Tawhid mosque, which they owned for over twenty-years when they arrived in America from their homeland Africa.

Both of his parents were dark yet smooth skin. His father was a short, slim, healthy African man with a low Caesar cut.

His mother, Elijah Khajid was beautiful with a nice toned body for her age and a nice set of pearly white teeth.

Today was the last day of Ramadan, which was a thirty-day fasting prescribed for Muslims all over the world to learn self-restraint and to be obedient to Allah.

Elijah and two other women were preparing the halal meal for their feast after they break their fast when the sun goes down.

Her husband was in the large prayer area praying with four other men making their *Asr,* the afternoon prayer.

Bloc!

Bloc!

Bloc!

Bloc!

Bloc!

Bloc!

Bloc!

Bloc!

All three almost jumped out their skin to the loud gunshots a few feet away.

Elijah stopped what she was doing and rushed to the open door. She saw three big white boys with their guns blazing. There was no doubt in her mind that her husband was dead and she was next.

"May Allah forgive you from the evil work," she said backing up as a short man walked in the kitchen area wearing a suit with tattoos on his baldhead.

"Who the fuck is Shaten and anybody ever tell you that you look like the black lady on the maple syrup bottle?" Sergio laughed.

"Yeah, your mother did," Elijah said showing no fear standing her ground as a strong Muslim woman.

"You're a tough nigger," Sergio said as he hog spit in her face. "You lucky I'm short on time or I would have my goon fuck you a new asshole. Kill all of them," he said walking out as gunshots could be heard, echoing through at the mosque and outside where their drivers awaited them.

Sergio walked past the four dead men. One he noticed from the picture inside Live's wallet he left at the shootout in co-op city last week.

One of Sergio's men picked up Live's wallet before he ran off to save his life. He gave his wallet to Sergio to find pictures of Live's parents and his I.D. with a mosque address on it.

Sergio had his men watching the mosque for four days and today was the day he made his checkmate.

*****

MDC, Brooklyn

Live was sitting in the pre-trial courtroom for his Fed case.

Two days ago, Live was driving by himself coming out of a shopping center parking to be ambushed by federal agents with gun with a SWAT team.

Live had a gun in his stash spot under the floor of his Camaro SS but by the time he would have gotten to that, he would have been dead.

After being arrested, he found out he was charged with five murders in the parking lot of a seafood restaurant in a co-op city.

He was sick and when he saw the evidence, he was sicker because all they had on him was his fingerprint on some of the shell cases.

With no witnesses, no footage, no statement, the feds did whatever they want and with a public defender, he knew he was alone.

His arresting officer was one of the baddest bitches he ever seen, and she had that Brooklyn swag he liked. Her name was Jamika.

He was denied bail because he was on parole and catching a new case is a violation.

Live didn't want to write, call or email Gunna yet because he knew the feds listened and monitored everything inmates did. The only thing he could do was wait and pray to Allah.

It was early in the morning. He was drinking a cup of coffee, thinking how many sets of pull ups, clips and push-ups he wanted to do. Whenever he came to jail, he used that time to get his mind and body right.

He heard the C.O. call his name in the dayroom. He was sitting next to a big muscle Muslim dude name Bama from Yonkers who just blew trial to three bodies. He was also his cellie.

"I am pull up on the C.O. real quick. Come with me," Live said as the big muscle Muslim man followed him.

"The chapel called you. Take your I.D. with you," the big ugly black older lady said as Live felt he had his ID in his pocket.

"I'm ready," Live said wondering what the fuck the chapel could want. Maybe it was about Ramadan's last feast in a couple of days where the Muslim in jail come together to eat a big meal

"Vin Diesel can't go with," she said making a call so the C.O. could escort Live to the Chapel because he was a high-profile inmate.

"Listen bitch, I got five life sentences. You got one more time to say some slick shit out your ratchet ass yak mouth. Live, holler at me when you get back. Hold your head," Boma said walking off as the C.O. chick looked scared.

*****

Minutes Later

Live walked into the chapel as two black correctional officers waited at the entrance door.

"You called me?" Live asked the old black man with gray hair and a gray beard in a suit. He was the jail pastor.

"Yes, I don't know how to pronounce your name. I'm sorry but I have very horrible news for you. Your parents were both gunned down in a mosque killing yesterday. It's been all over the news. I'm sorry, hate crimes are big these days," the pastor said.

Live only saw his lips move once he heard his parents were killed. He went deaf in both ears

"If you like, I can give you a private call. Just dial one it's a private line. I am giving you five minutes," the pastor said as he stood to leave the small office as Live held his tears back.

Live dialed Gunna's number and he picked up on the first ring.

"Gun" Live said when he picked up.

"Yo, bro where you been? Where you at?"

"They killed my parents," he stated in a soft voice holding back his emotion because he wanted to cry.

"Shhittt, son. Fuck, I'm sorry. I swear I'ma handle it but where are you?"

"MDA. The feds got me for a shot killing five people but it's bullshit," he said thinking about his parents.

"I knew something was up. I'ma get you a lawyer. Don't worry about nothing, son. I'ma take care of out here. You just hold your head."

"Facts. I love you," Live stated.

"Love you too," Gunna said hanging up.

"You good. I'm here if you need anything," the pastor said as Live just walked out being escorted back upstairs to the seventh floor.

"The coder went off in your unit, so when you go back inside, go straight to your cell," a young black C.O. told him as the got off the elevator.

Live heard a woman yelling, when he saw the fat C.O. woman who worked his block on a stretcher with her face cut wide open with a razor and two black eyes, he was shocked. Seconds behind her he saw Boma walking out with cuffs on yelling.

"I told that bitch. Yo, Live hold your head. Pack all my shit," Boma yelled as then officers forced him in the elevator and started to beat the shit out of him as Live walked on the empty unit, because everybody was locked in as he went to his cell crying.

Chapter Twenty

Yazd, Iran

Ariana was hiking into the rugged Yazd mountains in her marine uniform with a twenty pound backpack on with a vest as she marched with night vision goggles and AR 15 assault rifle.

Ariana was a part of the Special Ops Team in the middle East who hunted down dangerous terrorist leaders. She was one of the best fighters, shooters, and hunters in her unit, out training a lot of men.

She was beautiful light skin like her father Web, with bright hazel eyes, long jet black curly hair, dimples, toned, petite body type, standing five foot six in height, B cup breast, long eyelashes, nice lips and always got confused with the model, Draya from the *Basketball Wives* show.

At twenty-three years old, she had her life in order, but her life was now all about the Marines. Most people though she was a pretty girl not knowing she was a skillful killer.

Being raised in Atlanta, GA, was decent. She was raised by a single mother who owed two hair salons in zone six of Atlanta, where she grew up.

Growing up without a father was awkward at times, especially when father and daughter day at school, or her prom, her becoming an honor student, graduating high school and becoming a woman.

Luckily her mother, Katherine was a strong Dominican woman from Washington Heights, New York.

Ariana was Dominican and black. She saw pictures of her father and he was a very handsome man, so she knew where she got her looks from as well as her beautiful mother.

Every time she asked about her father, her mom told her very little except he is very powerful man, and he is the reason who they have a good life but she hadn't seen him in years.

Little did Ariana know, when Katherine was young, she stole two million dollars from Web and moved to Atlanta, only to find out she was pregnant with his daughter. Knowing how dangerous he was, she cut all ties to him, praying he would never find her as she opened two hair salons and raised her daughter.

Ariana was with a six-man crew of the best Special Ops Team. She was in the front as she stopped and raised her right hand up and painted three fingers to her right where she heard movement from.

Seeing a figure move in her night vision goggles, she fired towards the trees and bushes as shooters came out of trees shooting and from under leaves.

Tat.

Tat.

Tat.

Bloc.

Bloc.

Bloc.

Boc

Boc.

Boc.

It was a vicious gun battle as she took out four Iran terrorists dressed in black turbans. She saw their leader trying to hide behind a tree. Her team covered her as she swiftly duck walked towards Ali.

"Allah Akber," Ali shouted as Ariana shot him in the head three times as her and her team took out the rest of his crew and headed back down the mountain, which took them to sunrise.

*****

W South Beach, Miami

"It's so nice out here, baby. I can get use to this," Gabby said standing on the hotel balcony with a front row view of South Beach.

Gabby was standing on the balcony with a see-through Givenchy rope on with no panties or bra on as Tookie came up behind her in a tank top and shorts on.

"Enjoy it babe," he said as she turned around to face him rubbing his big, defined chest and broad shoulders.

"I love you," she said for the first time.

"You know you shouldn't say things you don't truly mean," he said seriously but smiling.

"I really do."

"I love you too," he said looking in her blue eyes as the Miami heat made his skin feel pure.

"I always wanted to suck dick on a balcony" said Gabby as she dropped to her knees and pulled his dick out and started to suck it.

Tookie saw people walking around downstairs on the streets, but he could care less. Gabby's head game made him feel like black bitches were the lowest creatures in life.

Gabby was twisting her head up and down until she felt him bang her throat with each bop as she sucked fast and slow. She was doing tricks with her two tongue rings as her couldn't take it no more.

"I'm cumming," he said, getting weak in his knees shooting cum in her warm mouth as she swallowed every drop and licking his tip while smiling at his massive dick.

"Come on, I'm going to make you tap out today," he said walking into her large bedroom as she dropped her robe showing her phat, pink pussy and phat ass that was soft and heavy. "I can take some dick," she said climbing in bed as she pulled at a camera recorder.

*****

Manhattan, NY

Tonight was Sergio's birthday and he just wanted to enjoy himself without a care or worry in the world.

He was in his Manhattan condo he paid $40,000 a month for. It was a sky raiser palace to him.

There was 170 grams of coke all over the glass table with rolled up dollars for his guest he was waiting for. Sergio wore a Versace robe naked under showing his hairy chest, dick and balls hanging out.

Sergio had four guards outside. They weren't allowed in his condo ever. Sergio was waiting on four black hookers to come so he could party.

For years, he had a thing for black women and hookers. He caught four STD's already, but he loved the hookers.

"Boss, the women are here," one of his guards yelled opening the condo door so they could walk in.

"Ladies come, come. Drinks at the bar over there and coke and weed right here. The pills and molly are on the kitchen table. Let's party. Money isn't an issue. All of you will be blessed tonight," Sergio said talking fast because he was high on coke.

"Oh, this nigga got Molly. I'ma fuck this white nigga all night," one of the girls shouted, popping a hand full of molly.

Sergio saw how two of them were extra thick. He couldn't wait to fuck them in their asses. He saw two skinny ones, but one of them was tall. She had thick lips. He planned to have that one such the life out of his dick.

"Redbone, come here," Sergio said to a thick redbone in a tight, dirty red dress with a pair of Wal-Mart heels on. "Suck me," he said sitting down as she did as she was told.

A thick dark skin chick hit two lines of coke and took off her dress as her breast sagged to her stomach.

"I wanna taste," the thick one said as she was sucking his head and deep throating like a magic trick as redbone sucked his balls

"Uhm, yeah. Long legs, come put your tongue in my ass," Sergio said as the two women was spitting and slurping on his dick as he moaned in ecstasy

Long legs put her drink down and walk over there with the other women. The other skinny woman started to such on Sergio's nipples as he closed his eyes in pleasure, but when he opened his eyes, he wished he would have kept them closed.

Long legs shot all three women in the head with a pistol with a silencer and now aimed it at Sergio as blood from the women was all over his body.

The hooker head collapsed his dick and Sergio panicked.

"Look we can talk about this. What do you want? Just put the gun down, baby. Please," Sergio protested, talking a 1000 mph.

"Shut up muthafucker," the woman said with a manly voice as Sergio looked shocked, but he had a feeling she was a tranny.

"Who sent you?" he said now sweating.

"Nigga I sent me. You killed my right hand's family. You thought you was safe and to make shit sad your sister, Gabby informed me how you love hookers, so I took it upon myself to pop up on you, freak muthafucker," Gunna said pulling off his wig throwing it on his face.

Gunna wore a fake wig, fake ass, fake breast make-up, nails toes done, he fooled many people tonight even one of the guards who slid him their number.

"That little bitch. I should of never stop raping that damn bitch. You got me good kid, but even when you kill me, it will never be over. I'm just a small fish," Sergio said laughing as if he was a manic.

"I guess I'll work my way up the food chain."

PSST.

PSST.

PSST.

PSST.

PSST.

PSST.

PSST.

Gunna shot him in the face seven times and put his wig back on.

When he made it in the hallway, he told the guard he was too freaky for his taste as they all laughed asking for his number, but

Gunna turned them down. They looked at his small ass all the way into the elevator disappeared.

Chapter Twenty-One

Caracas, Venezuela

Elena was in her country capital Caracas, which was beautiful bright city with a lot of oil revenues, livestock farms, and pharmaceutical companies.

She was sitting at the dinner room table, in her mansion having dinner with her nephew as his and her guards surrounding the house.

"Good to see you, Flaco. You grew into a handsome young man. How's business? I hear you took over your father's operations," Elena said looking beautiful in white, Alexander McQueen dress glowing in her diamond earrings, necklace, ring and watch.

"It's been a while Aunty, but everything is great."

"Please, don't call me Aunty. It makes me feel old, but my daughter asked about you last week. You know she is in college in the UK. She loves it," Elena said speaking of her 19-year beautiful daughter, Teresa, she loved to death.

"How is she?"

"Good grades and she wants to live in the UK, but I don't mind. It's better than the dirty States," Elana said taking a bite of grilled pork seasoned perfect with onions, green peppers, and chili peppers on it.

"How come you didn't come to my father's funeral? I know you to have your differences and what not but you're still family," Flaco said looking at his beautiful aunt whom he haven't seen in five years.

"I don't do funerals and your father was a piece of shit. I'm sorry but your father did a lot of fucked up shit to people. I guess that's why he died the way he did, Flaco. I loved Rafael but he had a lot of demons nobody knew about," she said sadly.

"I understand where you're coming from, but he was still my father and your brother and you know family means everything to the cartel."

"I agree. Hopefully we find his killers so we can at least let his soul rest peacefully," she said eating her dinner.

"I know who killed my father," he said as she stopped eating. "Before he died, he was telling me about a man who was hiding for a while and came back for blood, his blood. His name is Web."

"Web? Are you sure? From where?"

"Yes, he is from New York, but I heard he has a residence in Connecticut, but I hear he's a dangerous man and not to be slept on. I assume you know him."

"Yes, but just give me some time to figure this out."

"Okay, thank you for dinner. I hope you make the right choice. I'm sure my father would have done it for you," Flaco said before exiting her mansion with his men. Elena tossed her plate of food at her wall and screamed. She hated when shit came between her business. Especially a piece of shit like her brother who she hadn't talked to in over twenty years.

*****

Manhattan, NY

Carmilla was in the Manhattan Federal building where she was using a lieutenant's office for her case. She was treated like a boss because she was head of Federal buildings except in D.C., her main headquarters.

She had just got off the phone with her boss who was telling her to speed up her investigation because he felt as if the case was better than the Mafia.

It didn't take long to connect the dots of all the murders going on with the Mob and Web's son. His crew had their name all over it and she knew Web was the one sending the hits. He was a mastermind. That's what made him so successful.

Carmilla had to do something quick. Especially after seeing the news this morning of Sergio, the capo being gunned down in his condo with some hookers.

*****

Bridgeport, CT

Murda was in the gym area lifting 305 pounding on the flat bench press, with no spot. He had an old LOX album booming through the speakers.

Web was doing weighted pull-up with a belt and fifty dumbbells hanging from his waist on his twenty-five rep

Both men were sweating and done with their two-hour exercise routine.

"Come upstairs real quick, son," Web said grabbing two new clean white towels tossing him one to wipe his sweat off before walking into the house.

Ten guards surrounded on the house on this nice afternoon. Everybody had plans to go out to Vegas on Web's jet to celebrate his forty-first birthday this weekend.

Murda followed his dad into his office while putting on his Givenchy tank top. He met with Gunna last night as he informed him on the event on Sergio. Murda couldn't help but laugh when he heard what he did but when he heard what happen to Live's parents, his heart went out to him.

Hearing Live being arrested for five bodies made him nervous, but he knew Live was a stand-up kid. He made sure he had the best lawyer money could buy and he was well taken care of.

Once in Web's conference office, he sat down across from his pops in the Fendi Casa chair.

"Look at this," Web said handing him four photos as he took a seat.

"Damn, she's beautiful. Who is she? Shorty in the army?" Murda said looking at the pictures of a beautiful red bone. She was bad. He could tell she had a little Spanish in her like every Bronx girl.

"That's your sister, Ariana. She's in the Marines overseas. She grew up in Atlanta. Her mother stole a lot of money from me when we were young and skipped town, but I'm over that. I've been keeping an eye on her for years, but I think I'm ready to meet her. What you think?" Web asked his son.

"Go for it pops. We're grown kids now. I'm sure she will forgive you like I did for the time missed."

"I hope so."

"Where is she?" Murda questioned, as they both heard gun fire interrupting their father and son bond.

Web turned on his computer screen with cameras surrounding the mansion to see it was an ambush with men coming from everywhere.

"Fuck, damn it. Put this on," Web said tossing him a bullet-proof vest from under his desk and he placed one on also. He ran to his closet and grabbed two hundred round clips AL-47. "We gotta get to the speed boat. Come on. I'ma see what you made of now," Web said exiting the room with Murda on his heels.

Tut.

Tut.

Tut.

Tut.

Tut.

Tut.

Tut.

Tut.

Tut.

Web shot the Spanish gunmen left in right as Murda did the same as they were now in the middle of the hall shooting every Spanish gunman came through the door or out the cut.

Two Spanish men popped out a closet in the hallway, hitting Murda in his arm as Murda shot before of the men in the head dropping them.

"Come on, follow me," Web said running towards the back stepping over bloody dead bodies over the place.

Four shooters were in the kitchen coming in from the back but Murda and Web killed them before they could even let off a shot.

"Duck," Murda yelled to Web as two gunmen snuck up behind them from the laundry room. He shot them in their upper torso, as they stumbled backwards into the laundry room.

Once out back, Web thought they were in a safe zone, until gunmen climbed out the pool shooting and from the roof.

"Cover me," Web yelled shooting the seven gunmen snipping from the roof as Murda was going toe to toe in a vicious gun battle, killing twelve gunmen as they finally made it to the dock were there speedboat was.

"Look out," Murda shouted as he shot the gunmen who popped up in the speed boat from the floor with an assault rifle.

Tut.

Tut.

Tat.

Murda shot the man in his private area as he screamed out in pain.

"Who sent you?" Murda said pointing his AK at the man's forehead.

"Elena and Flaco sent us to kill Web," the man cried in pain

"Too bad," Web said shooting the man four times in the head and tossing him off the boat as shots was being sent in their direction.

"Go, go, go…" Web told Murda as he raced off in the speed boat while Web was still letting off shots towards the gunmen running towards the dock.

"That fucking bitch."

"Whose Elena?" Murda asked taking off his vest and tank top tying it around his arm where he was shot at.

"The Venezuelan Cartel and my plug. Flaco is Rafael's son. I don't know what's going on, but I'ma find out soon."

Chapter Twenty-Two

Months Later

Jamika was frozen as she climbed out of her Lexus rushing into her downtown Brooklyn apartment.

Work had been crazy and confusing for her lately since Sergio was found brutally murdered in his condo.

She had a no idea who did it, but this threw a twist in her case and now the big question for her boss was who killed Sergio.

Wintertime in New York was ice cold with snow so high your socks, sneakers, and pants would be soaked.

Jamika wore a Saint Laurent peacoat with her FBI hoodie under as she entered the lobby, pulling out her keys to see a man with a Gucci hoodie and Gucci winter boots standing in her lobby.

"What you want and what are you doing here?" Jamika said sharply with an upset face looking at Murda.

"I came to talk to you," he said.

"At my home? Are you fucking serious?"

"Yea, I am serious about you," he said stepping close to her as one of her nosey neighbors came off the elevator with a laundry bag.

"Hey Jamika, you ok?" an old white lady with glasses and a gown on showing her saggy wrinkle breast asked, going downstairs in the laundromat to wash clothes.

"Yes, Mrs. Aldenson," Jamika said showing a fake smile so she would go away. "Oh my G,od come upstairs," Jamika said letting out a deep breath as they got in her elevator.

This was her first time bringing over a male to her home but something about Murda made her feel at ease even though she knew he was a killer.

"Nice crib," Murda said walking into her polish apartment as he stepped down the stairs leading into the living room where he took a seat.

"Thanks, now what do you want?" she shouted from her kitchen.

"I don't get offered nothing to drink? I'm your guest," Murda said being funny.

"There is a bar down the block," Jamika said walking into the living room with her heels off, slacks, and a blouse.

Murda looked at her nice round breast and curves, surprised she was holding like that.

"Look, I know you doing your job but why did you arrest Live for them bodies?" he asked.

"It was my case. I was doing my job."

"No, you saw the dead mobsters and framed him because you knew was down with me," said Murda.

"I don't give a fuck if he was down with Obama care. You do a crime, then you go to jail. You're just a lucky one. Two cop killings, over twenty bodies, let's not forget, a drug lord," she said counting on her fingers.

"Jamika, what evidence do you or your people have on me? I'm not dumb. I know how to move. Whatever you are finding, it won't stick."

"I'll make it stick," she stated smiling, loving this game he was playing as if he was innocent. "I'm surprised you or your team got close to Sergio. How you do it? Dressed up as a hooker or something?" she said with a laugh.

"I didn't come here for that. I came to ask you about Live but I'm out," he said standing to leave.

"Bye."

"The crazy part is I'm really feeling you, Jamika. You haven't left my mind since the first day I laid eyes on you," he said as she stood up to walk him out.

"I'm a cop. You don't know me, Jamel."

"I know you love purple, exercise every morning at five a.m., your left handed, you sleep with your lights on, you love animals, you're a vegan, you're a real woman, your beautiful and you're everything I ever wanted in life, and I would give up everything to have you," he said as she was now weak in the knees.

"I want you too," she said softly shocked those words escaped her mouth.

Murda kissed her and she grabbed him, attacking him, feeling his muscular rock-hard body. She pulled off his hoodie and his V-neck t-shirt looking at his six pack and his bullet wound as she touched it.

"Ssss," He moaned. They kissed more before walking to the couch, both horny as ever.

Jamika stripped down ass naked, showing her round perky firm breast and waxed brown pussy with her clit peeking out as she was wetter than a river.

"I wanna taste you," Murda said sitting her down and tossing her toned legs over his shoulders, bringing him face to face with her phat, pretty, soft pussy.

Murda circled her clit with his warm tongue, as a sexual electricity shocked her body as she thrusted her hips into his face.

"Uhm please, Oh," she moaned as he lightly sucked on her pussy lips. He traced small circles around her swollen clit as she went crazy.

Murda knew he had her right where he wanted her, as his tongue massaged her pussy walls.

"Ugh fuck baby, I'm about to , ugh. Shh," she cried out nutting all over her couch as her watery cream was dripping on her carpet.

Murda sat he up on the couch and pulled out his long hard beefy dick and entered her warm tight cave as she grabbed his big arms.

"Ssss, yesss daddy," she moaned. She felt his rod inside her juicy sex box as he slowly stroked, opening her walls.

"Damn you got some fire," Murda said as his dick was trying to tell him to bust but his mind told him no.

Within seconds, Jamika was riding his dick like a wild girl as she has bouncing her hips into his dick.

"Fuck me!!! Harder, harder, oh fuck," she screamed as he gripped her hips and started to pound her pussy out continuing he hit the bottom of her pussy.

Once he came, she came seconds later on his dick then she tasted it sucking his dick like a blow pop.

Jamika then slid up and down on his pole riding him while he sucked her little Hershey Kiss nipples, as her ass clapped up and down on his thighs.

"Uhmmm," Murda moaned grabbing a handful of her wide ass cheeks spreading them apart giving her wet pussy inches as his dick almost knocked her heart out of place.

"I'm cumming, oh shit" Jamika yelled biting her lips still bouncing on his dick sitting and grinding it as she felt the spasms in her body. "Come to the bedroom," Jamika said as she stood up and fell over on the ground and started to laugh as Murda helped her up.

"Talk that gangsta shit now," Murda said carrying here to the room in the back.

"You got that, big daddy. Hope you not tired," she said as she was ready to perform.

"Never," he said tossing her on her bed bending her over to see mirrors on the ceiling and walls as he went to work.

They fucked and fell asleep, not believing they both just cross the line.

*****

Brooklyn Federal Court
Days Later

Live sat in the cold, dirty smelly bullpen eating processed bologna and cheese sandwiches with seven other inmates waiting to see the judge.

"Yo kid, with the weird African name. Someone wants to see before you see the judge," an agent stated

"Put some respect on my name and I don't want to see no DA for no meetings or one on one. 5KL someone else, dickhead," Live shouted to the guard standing outside the gates.

"You got a slick mouth on you kid and it's not the DA. You coming or not?" the tall agent asked with old rusty cuffs out.

“Aight,” Live said walking to the gate to get cuffed with his hands behind his back.

Live was brought to a small booth area behind a glass to see the bad ass agent bitch who charged him for five bodies.

“Good morning,” she said wearing glasses sitting calmly with a notepad and pen.

“What the fuck you want?” Live said pissed.

“Look, I come in peace. I’m here to make a deal. Give me some names of people you know going at it with the mafia, because I know you had something to do with it. So, give me names and you go free today as long as it checks out,” Jamika stated looking at Live laugh at her

“Where I’m from, that’s called snitching and you got the wrong nigga. I don’t talk that language. They can hit me with ten elbows, the chair, 500 years, it’s my destiny so tell the guards to send me back to the bullpen,” Live stated calmly.

“You sure?” Jamika asked as Live got up to knock the door so he could leave.

“Don’t ever call me down here again, you stupid bitch.

“Fuck you too. Don’t drop the soap, bum nigga,” Jamika said standing to leave.

“You can’t drop something you don’t got, bum bitch. That’s why your tracks are uneven,” Live yelled as she slammed the door on her way out. The agents came and brought Live back to the bullpen. He knew his life was over but seeing Sergio dead in the newspaper made him feel better because he knew he killed his parents.

Chapter Twenty-Three

Manhattan, NY

Web was in his office in the Web Lounge thinking about how Elena and Rafael's son came together to end his life, but they needed more manpower.

Web heard his office phone ring taking him out of his trace of thoughts.

"Sir you have a visit from Ms. Chelsea and a couple of men with her. Should we let her in or send her on her way?" the security guard asked through the phone.

"Let her up," he said hanging up, wondering what the fuck his dead brother's wife wanted.

Minutes later, Chelsea walked in wearing a long Louis Vuitton slit dress that dragged on the ground.

"Webster, good to see you again," she said walking in like a diva as her goons waited outside the office.

"How may I help you, Chelsea?"

"The place looks the same. You got good taste," Chelsea stated looking outside his window.

"What do I owe this visit too?" Web said as she turned around to him.

"You been a bad boy, Web. Your name is all the way in Italy. I never knew you had a son and a handsome one at that," Chelsea said walking over to his bar to pour herself a drink.

"I see Donvito is grooming you good, but what made you get into your family business? I never saw you as the type. Well, at least not when you were with Chris," Web said.

"The mafia is just in my blood. When I fell in love with Chris, I was a young girl and now, I'm grown woman," she said sexually licking her lips at him.

"Why are you here? I don't deal with Mobsters."

"Get use to this Mobster face because soon I'ma be over all the families if Joe doesn't kill you by the," she said with a chuckle.

"Congratulations you want a cookie? At least you ain't have to fuck your way to the top. Maybe just cross and kill your loved ones."

"Only if you knew," she said smiling.

"I'm sure, but I have a meeting to attend to," Web stated.

"I just came to pay you a visit, sexy. How was your birthday weekend? I heard you and yours went out blasting like the D.C. sniper," Chelsea stated making guns pop with her hands.

"How do you know about that?"

"I know everything. I even know you have a big nice dick that I would love to taste," she said approaching him.

"Never."

"Never say never. I always get what I want, trust daddy," She said seriously sitting on his desk showing him her legs and thighs.

"What do you know, Chelsea? Enough of these games," Web said standing up walking in the front of her between her legs spreading them open.

"I don't know nothing, Webster," she said cocking her legs open more.

Web moved her thong to the side and rammed two fingers into her pussy as she squirmed.

"Uhmmmm," she said grabbing on to the edge of the desk as Web fingered her moist pussy.

"Tell me," he said in her ear.

"Elenaaa is Rafael's sister. Ohhh shit, I'm cummmminggg ugh," she yelled as she came on his fingers. Chelsea grabbed his fingers and sucked his fingers clean as if she was sucking a dick.

"Get the fuck out," Web said opening the door for her.

"Thank you. See you later," Chelsea started slowly walking out laughing.

*****

Bogota, Colombia

Carmilla was just cleared to enter her little brother's mansion by his guards to see Colombian women run around in bikinis.

Carmilla shook her head as she made her way to his basement area where he had an inside pool.

Downstairs, there were naked women in the pools as loud Latina music played throughout the large basement that was the size of a house itself

Flaco was in the pool with six sexy women sniffing coke and drinking, having the time of his life.

Carmilla wore a white Versace skirt, a top and heels with sunglasses on as she walked to her brother.

"Sister, wow good to fucking see you. If it ain't Ms. FBI herself," Flaco said clapping his hands as a woman went under water to suck his dick as she was high on ecstasy.

"Flaco, can I please talk to you?" Carmilla stated as she watched the woman suck his dick like a porn star under water.

"Okay, ok, ok," he said lifting the pretty young chick head up from under the water before he climbed out.

Flaco wrapped a towel around his body and walked his sister to a private storage room next to his shower room.

"Flaco, this isn't you," Carmilla yelled to his little brother whom she helped raised.

"This is me now. What the fuck do you want coming down here and you couldn't even come to our father's funeral," Flaco shouted in pain and because he was high.

"You know how I felt about him," she replied in Spanish.

"It doesn't matter."

"It does because Rafael killed our fucking mother," she shouted with tears because she tried to keep it a secret from him. Carmilla saw Rafael kill her mother one morning, and her father spoke nothing of it.

"Why are you just telling me this?" he said in Spanish.

"Because I wanted to protect your feelings."

"Too late now. I have no feelings."

"What's up with this war you have going on?"

"You mean a war with the men who killed our father? Your husband? You're lucky if I even let you walk out this house," Flaco said in Spanish.

"Flaco, this is a war you will not win. This man is dangerous. Please, stop. Let Rafael rest. I don't want you to be next," Carmilla said honestly already knowing Web was on a kill mission and won't stop until bloodlines are wiped out.

"Carmilla, this is the Cartel. We live for wars and death. Me and Elena are going to kill your husband and if you get in the way, then you're dead as well," Flaco stated in Spanish getting pissed pointing a finger in her face.

"Okay Flaco. Well, I'm riding with my husband so do what you got to. I'll see you in hell," Carmilla stated walking out the room in tears but he had to choose a side if she couldn't bring peace.

Carmilla loved Web and this proved it she was willing to turn on her family for a man who kidnapped her.

Carmilla left the mansion and headed back to New York to do some more research on this Joe case since Sergio was whacked.

Chapter Twenty-Four

Zahedan, Iran

Ariana was in the backseat of a military tank with four other solders on their way to Chah Bahar, Iran, eighty miles west of their station.

It was one in the afternoon and the desert heat was so vicious. Heat waves danced outside their windows.

The tank was driving on the dirt back roads. They always took the back roads for safety precautions.

Ariana was on her iPhone texting a male friend she had known for a while when the RV tank, blew up killing the driver and passenger. Everybody else was able to crawl out.

Her team and her started to shoot at the two black SUVs, until four smoke bombs went off causing loud explosions.

The rest of her team was gunned down by the eight shooters dressed in all black with vests and assault rifles.

Ariana was unable move as the smoke bomb took her last breath before she passed out unconscious near the RV.

The gunmen grabbed Ariana, placed her in their truck, and pulled off before another RV was able to come.

*****

The C.O. just told Live he had a visit, as he was in small in-door rec area doing push-ups and burpees with his man Day Day Loc from Crown Heights.

"I'ma go get ready, boy. I'ma pull up on you when I get back son," Live said as he walked inside the unit to change out his grey sweat suit into brown overalls.

Live been in the Federal hold over for months now awaiting trial. He recently got his $3,500 Brandy material containing his case, which was mainly all the evidence they had on him.

His paid lawyer told him he had a good chance of beating his case, but he knew most lawyers told all of their clients the same thing.

Financially, Murda and Gunna made sure he was straight. His account was at the max at $99,999. He got close a rookie female C.O. and she was bringing him in drugs and phones.

Live was waiting on an escort to his visit because he was a high-profile case so they had to stop all inmate movement for him.

His old cellie Boma from Yonkers was shipped off to a USP in Kentucky called Big Sandy to do his time he promised to keep in touch with the crazy nigga because he was official.

On the visit floor, which inmates called the dance floor was filled with families and friends there to show their support to their love ones.

Live saw Gunna sitting at the second-round table near the C.O. booth so he could be watched.

"Yo…what's good boy" Gunna told Live as both men embraced each other before sitting down.

"Bro these crackers trying to roof a nigga," Live said shaking his head.

"I already know, blood. Everything's going to fall in place soon. Just stay focused and sucker free in the belly of the beast."

"This shit is really the belly of the sheep. These niggas ratting like they life depend on it, son. I gotta get my time and keep it pushing."

"Facts, but it may not even go that far." Live said nothing already knowing his fate.

"Good looks on that situation, bro. I don't know how you did it, but you did," Live stated talking about him killing Sergio.

"Shit is crazy out there right now. It's nasty in the town," Gunna stated seriously.

"So, I heard fam."

"Guess what bro? You ain't going to believe this, but you have to keep it on the cool soon, because it could come in your favor," Gunna said in a low pitch voice.

"What?"

"You know shorty who arrested you?"

"Yeah that grimy bitch."

"Well that's Murda's wifey now bro. I don't know how the fuck that happened, but he in love with ole girl," Gunna stated as Live looked shocked.

"Wow."

"He asked about you, but he is pushing for you, Live. Just hold your head and keep faith son," Gunna stated as Live couldn't believe the news.

Live and Gunna talked for another hour before there visit was over.

*****

Miami, FL

Tookie and Gabby were on South Beach lying in the hot tar sand enjoying the Miami heat because right now in New York it was a snowstorm.

"I love it out here, baby," Gabby said in her two pieced Fendi bikini showing her flat stomach and thick body that made every nigga stare as they walked past.

"Let's buy a house out here, then," Tookie stated her lying next to her shirtless flexing his abs, chest, and big arms as people thought he was a bodybuilder.

"You can't be serious?" she said.

"You pick it and it's ours, baby. You deserve it. You gave up your life to be with me on some Bonnie and Clyde shit," Tookie said making her laugh.

"Bonnie and Clyde huh/? I like that," she said kissing his lips watching their jet skis tear up the South Beach water as people enjoyed themselves.

Every night was a party night for the two clubs, dinners, events, concerts, and big parties. No one had a clue they were on the run as they both raced Rolls Royce Wraiths up and down Collin Ave.

When people asked what they did for a living. Gabby stated she was a model and Tookie was a personal trainer for famous clients and people bought it.

"I have something to tell you, daddy," Gabby said in her sweet voice looking him in his dark eyes she loved.

"What's up? Don't tell me you were born a man," Tookie said making her laugh as she slapped him on his wide chest.

"Baby, for real. I'm, uh, five to six weeks pregnant. I'm sorry. I didn't know but I will..."Tookie cut her off kissing her, already knowing what she was about to say and he was against abortions.

"I love you baby. This will make us whole now," he said as she looked shocked because this was everything, she wanted.

"Okay," she said in her white girl voice.

"No more killing."

"Okay, but we should be good out here. Nobody would ever find us out here. There's too many people," she said looking around at the large crowds of people from all races all over the beach.

"I hope that's the case, but let's get out of here and go shopping. You know I got this black card," he said flashing it as they got up to leave.

Chapter Twenty-Five

Midtown, NY

Web recently rented a condo downtown until he found a new mansion outside of New York. He was thinking about New Jersey or somewhere upstate New York.

There was so much going on, Web forgot he needed to find his son a connect since Elena jumped ship and double crossed him.

After hearing the news of Elena being Rafael's sister, he felt dumb for not doing his full research on Elena. He was blinded by her beauty and business.

He knew she could be a big threat if he didn't push the issue fast. She already almost took his life and his son he refused to let that happen again.

Security was extra tight, and he was war ready for whatever else comes his way.

Web did a little research on Elena and found out she had a daughter in Paris already in college, and she was also once married.

Rafael introduced him to Flaco many times. He knew he lived a party lifestyle and lived in the capital of Colombia, Bogota.

Web saw his business phone ringing, but it was a FaceTime call. He had no clue who it was as he answered it.

Web saw a video of a dark room, but he saw nobody. Seconds later, Elena appeared smiling wearing a nice little black dress as she sat in a chair surrounded by a group of mask men.

"Mr. Web good to see you. I'm sure you know what going on now. You killed someone dear to me," she said holding her heart.

"Life goes on but what do you want? I hope you didn't call me to beg for your life so quick," he replied.

"Sexy and dangerous, I love a man of your status. Too bad it has to end this way. I had plans one day to let you fuck me really good. What a shame," she stated.

"I wouldn't fuck you with a horse dick."

"That's how I like it, Web, but enough of the flirting. I have something of yours for your life," she said seriously.

"What's that?" Web said as the phone camera went to a woman tied up inside of a dog cage with her mouth duct taped.

Web knew who the woman as soon as he saw her. It was Ariana.

"I'm give you seventy-two hours to come to my home come alone, and Web, as they say in America. Checkmate," she said laughing as she hung up.

Web banged his fist on his living room table. He was pissed Elena outsmarted but he had a trick up his sleeve as he made a call.

*****

Paris, France

Teresa walked through her college dorm hallways, greeting other students as they just stood around talking in their French language.

She attended the famous Paris School of Art. It was one of the most expensive colleges to get in but lucky her mother Elena was rich.

Teresa worked at the college radio, France International, five days a week. Everything from rap, rock, and of course pop, her favorite.

She was beautiful, just like her mother. She looked foreign with her white skin complexion, blonde hair, green and gray bright eyes, big ears, thin lips, small breast A cups, a nice small petite frame with an ample plump round ass.

Teresa walked into the school parking lot feeling her phone vibrate as she pulled it out to see she got a text from her boyfriend, who was black from Haiti.

She had a thing for blacks. Not only was their dick game the best, but their physiques made her go crazy.

She sent him a text saying she couldn't wait to such his dick with a smiley face emoji.

It was a dark cool winter windy night in Paris. It was never to cold or snowy in the winter. It was perfect.

Her new Lotos Evara 400 with a pink custom-made paint job was parked ten feet away from

A van approached her from behind as she looked and continued to walk.

Teresa heard footsteps as if someone was running behind her, which made her calmly look back.

When she saw five big black men rushing her, she screamed in took off towards the end of the parking lot, which was a dead end.

Two of the men was able to tackle her on to the floor as she was screaming, kicking and biting. She was able to kick one of the kidnappers in his nuts as she tried to get away and save her life.

The men were able to get her in the van as they placed a rag covering her face with strong chemicals on it that made her go to sleep like a baby.

Teresa woke up hours later tied up, sitting on a chair in a private jet fill of goons and a handsome light skin man.

She remembered everything that happened. She heard of women being kidnap and tortured. She started to silently pray.

"You're safe, Teresa. You don't have to panic," Web said looking into the nineteen-year-old eyes who looked just like Elena.

"What's going on? Please, let me go," she cried.

"I'm sorry, young lady. I can't until your mother gives me back my daughter."

Teresa knew it was because of her mom's dangerous lifestyle that she was kidnapped and tied up on a jet.

"I have nothing to do with it," she said in her strong Spanish accent.

"I'm sorry, but you do," Web said as he took her iPhone and looked for her mom's name and he found it right under Mama.

Web FaceTime'd Elena and she answered fast.

"Baby, how are you? Mommy misses you. How's school?" Elena said as she saw nothing but a floor view on her camera Facetime. "Teresa are you there?"

"Hello, Elena," Web said smiling into the phone.

"Oh my God. No! Where is my baby?" Elena cried

"She is here, but I believe you have something of mine and I have something of yours," Web stated.

"Where is she?"

"Right here," Web stated placing the video on Teresa.

"Mom, please help me. Give him what he wants please," Teresa yelled.

"You hear that?"

"Web don't lay a single hand on her or you will regret it."

"Save the tough talk for someone else. Now how do you want to do this? You got a pretty little daughter so I'm give you seventy-two hours to figure it out," Web said now hanging up in her face, smiling loving when the tables turn.

"You're going to kill me?" she asked shaken looking him in his deep hazel eyes.

"Just chill, you're ok. Trust me. If I wanted you dead, you would have been dead," he stated in a non-threating voice as she felt more comfortable hearing that.

"What's your name Mr.?" she asked.

"Web."

"I've heard of you. My mom always said how sexy you were. I see why now," she said closing her eyes to take a nap. Web shook his head. *Like mother like daughter* he thought to himself.

*****

New Orleans

Jamika just walked into a small shack near a swamp off the highway.

The shack had all types of Voodoo dolls, dead animals, animal eyes in jars, candles, toys, beaded drapes and wood clean floors.

Jamika came all the way down south to see a fortune teller. This was her first time, but her best friend Robin came with her, but she refused to go inside because outside looked creepy to her.

"Hello. Anybody here?" She said walking through the small home.

"Yes, Jamika. Come to the back please," said an older woman.

Jamika walked to the back confused as to how did the woman in the back knew her name. She was a surprise visit.

Once she walked through the long beads, she saw an old black woman sitting at the table playing with cards with her eyes closed and a head wrapped around her head covering her dreads, that dropped to the floor.

"Have a seat, please. Thank you for coming. I see you have a lot of worries on your mind," the woman said who was from Uganda.

"Yes, I do. How do you know?" She sat down as the woman finally opened her eyes almost scaring the life out of Jamika.

The woman eyes were bright orange as if they weren't real. Jamika never saw eyes of such color.

"Drink this," the old woman said passing her a cup of tea.

Jamika drank the cup and placed $500 on her table near her set of cards. The old woman pushed the money back to her.

"First time is free."

"Thank you."

"Place your hands out," the woman asked as Jamika did as she was told, watching the woman trace her lines in her inner hand. "Uhm," she moaned with her eyes closed. "I see you have a very dark future. You will be stuck in the rapture of love, but something will come to you then darkest will snatch it. There will be a lot of death around you soon. I see a lot of blood," she said opening her eyes as Jamika snatched her hand back and ran out the as the woman shouted something in her language while laughing loud as Jamika hopped in her car and speed off.

Chapter Twenty-Six

Brooklyn Federal Court

Live was sitting upstairs in a bullpen in an Armani blue suit waiting to see the judge, Mr. Westwood who was a fair middle age white man.

Live's lawyer kept his fingers crossed but he informed him they had a good chance of winning trial today.

Gunna told him he would be there in a limo to pick him up when he was freed, making him feel positive and strong. He was going to beat the hardest justice system.

The door opened and he saw two court Marshalls dressed in suits looking at him.

"You ready killer?" one of them asked laughing.

"The only thing I plan to kill is your daughter's pussy."

"You got one more fucking time kid, I'm telling you," the agent yelled as his face turn beat red as his partner laughed.

"Paul, I gotta go outside, please," his partner said as Paul walked through the court door on fire.

"Sucker nigga."

"Kid, you know his daughter just married a black dude so he's a little uptight," the agent said as he opened the bullpen so he could go see the judge. He was the only inmate ready to see the judge.

When Live walked into the courtroom, it was bright, wall to wall carpet, wood tables and benches for guest and criminals.

Live saw nobody he knew in the benches so he paid the couple of people no mind.

"How do you pronounce your last name again?" his lawyer asked as Live took a seat next to him.

"Kamagwazanele," Live said calmly as the DA and judge stared at him awkwardly.

"Is the court ready?" the judge asked sitting at the top of his throne.

"Ummm not really Judge Westwood. We have a big problem it seems all the evidence we did have of Mr. Ka-a-ma-g---whatever his name is has disappeared off the files and the bullets that we recovered somehow didn't match the same gun he used."

"What?" the judge shouted as Live's lawyer even looked crazy not believing what he was hearing.

"I'm sorry but if you give us some time, I'm sure we can find something on him or build something," The DA stated sounding thirsty.

"Mr. Loamas are you out your mind. This court isn't a playground. We have serious cases we have to attend to," the judge stated.

"Yes sir. I'm sorry."

"Mr. Kamagwazanele, this case is dismissed. You're free to leave. I'm very sorry for the mistake," the judge states as he banged his gravel then standing to leave tell Mr. Loamas to come to the back.

Live was so shocked and happy. His heart ain't stop racing yet.

"You got God on your side. I never saw nothing like that in my thirty years as a lawyer," Live's lawyer said as he shook his hand.

"It's the creed of Allah," Live said walking out the court as the two court Marshalls ice grilled him, hoping the judge would have nailed him as he did every young black man that sat in front of him.

Live stepped outside and wanted to kiss the floor as he inhaled the fresh air happy to be free.

Live saw a Bentley limo parked in front of the courthouse with an older white man hold the door open for him as if he was someone famous.

It was icy outside today from the recent snowstorm but Live didn't care as he rushed in the limo and told the driver to take him to East New York. He was sure Gunna would be over there. Live knew Gunna hated coming anywhere near police buildings or court. He thought that was bad luck. That's why when he come to see him, he was shocked.

Live was looking out the windows as the limo drove through downtown. The limo came to a stop at a red-light.

"You thought you was safe nigger," the driver said as he turned around with a gun with a silencer pointed at him.

"Fuck you bitch",

"Fuck you," Joe said shooting Live in his head five times then driving back to his limo company.

Early this morning, Joe was at his limo service doing some documents when he got a call from a man ordering a limo for a Kamaguazende and Joe remember seeing Live's face on the news and that was his last name.

Joe paid him an in person visit. He hadn't put in work in some years. He felt as if he was back to his yang self again.

*****

Bogota, Colombia

Flaco was just coming back from a big party full of drugs and women. It was his type of scene.

Flaco rode in a SUV with two Latina women on his side, ready for the after party as another SUV truck tailed him fill of soldiers heading back to his mansion.

Life been great for the boss. He was moving weight all over the globe. He felt as if he was untouchable. Now, he knew how his pops felt.

Flaco couldn't believe Carmilla told him she was about to pick the side of the man who killed their father.

He vowed the next time he saw her. He would put a bullet in her head without hesitation.

The truck road down the dark rocky Bogota roads unaware of three vans that turned off a side road following them with their lights off.

Flaco was kissing on one of the women's neck while the other one had his dick in her mouth before the truck was smashed from the back, forcing it off road.

The other SUV full of Flaco's goons was flipped over as two vans slammed into it.

"It's a hit get out."

Tat.

Tat.

Tat.

Tat.

Tat.

Tat.

Loud powerful bullets ripped through both SUVs as Flaco hopped up to see over thirty gunmen airing out the other SUV.

Flaco saw it was no winning and ran in the grass leading into the woods as bullets waved by his head.

Murda saw his truck target trying to get away and he chased him down with bullets.

Two bullets hit Flaco's butt cheeks making him fall face first into some leaves as he cried in pain.

"Cartel boss trying to run?" Murda said standing over him with a draco pointing at him.

"The cartel will live on," Flaco said in pain.

"Not today bay," Murda said shooting him seventeen times in his face.

Murda was in Bogota for two weeks showing up at the most live parties looking for Flaco because his pops told him he was a party head.

When he saw him tonight, he knew it was time.

Murda's security guard passed him a saw and Murda started to cut Flaco's neck off because Web wanted his head for some reason, and he promised to bring it to him.

Chapter Twenty-Seven

Manhattan, NY

Web just got off the elevator on his floor. Murda just texted him saying job done. He was pleased because he knew Flaco would be a headache.

When Web got to his door, he could tell it was played with or someone broke into his spot.

He had six guards with him. He gave them a look telling them to go in and do their job as he pulled out a 50 cal cannon ready to blow someone head off.

The guards busted in the condo and was yelling to someone to put their hands up.

Web walked in to see it was Carmilla standing in the middle of his living room floor with her hands up.

"She good. Y'all can leave," Web said staring at Carmilla in her blouse and gray por skirt.

"You sure boss?"

"Yes, thank you," Web took off his Talla blazer and tossed it on his Verscocer couch.

"I'm sorry for coming in this way but…"

"What do you want Carmilla?" Web said face to face with her smelling her Coach perfume

"They're going to try to kill you, Elena and Flaco," she said as he laughed.

"Oh, that's it?"

"Webster this isn't funny. Your life is at risk. I went to see him and he made me pick a side and I picked my husband so I'm just as dead as you are," she said as Web walked over to his bar to pour himself a drink.

"You want to drink? You're going to need it."

"What?" she said as her phone rang. It was one of her older cousins in Bogota. She told her how Flaco was found murdered on the road with his head cut off. She was at a loss for words as she hung up.

Carmilla couldn't believe what she heard. She had to sit down as Web brought her over a glass of wine.

"You ok?"

"I'm next?" she asked.

"No never. I can never kill something I love," he said moving her long hair out her face. Carmilla gulped her glass of wine in one sip as Web got up to get her another one.

"I'm sorry, Carmilla but this is life."

"I know, I just hope your love is worth it."

"Is it?" Web said kissing her lips as shit got hot quick and one thing led to the next and they both were in his bedroom naked.

Web hated to fuck raw but Carmilla was his wife. He had her on all fours as his massive large perfect shape dick was slamming in her tight pussy.

He was thrusting his dick in and out her back as she threw her ass back making it clip on his dick.

"Ugh, fuck me papi," she screamed. Web pumped harder and harder as her pussy muscles squeezed his dick. I'm cummmminggg," she yelled as she came uncontrollably as she let out deep, hard moans.

When he pulled out, she turned her attention to his cock, licking up one side and down the opposite side before softly lapping her long tongue over and under his balls sack.

Carmilla slid her lips up on his shaft and taking as much dick as she could in her mouth then she started to deep throat with ease.

Soon the head of his dick was overflowing with precum that oozed out as she caressed his dick with her mouth.

She was ready to fuck before he came so she laid on her back and placed her legs in the air, showing him the pretty little pussy, she knew he missed.

Web slowed place his penis in her pussy halfway as she went crazy

"Oh yeah, go deeper papi. Please fuck me," she yelled as Web started to fuck her pussy as she arched her lower body to feel all of his dick.

"Mmmmm," Web moaned as her pussy felt so good.

"Deeper, deeper. Fuck me with that big dick. Umm I love you," she yelled as she continued to yell for him to fuck her.

The claps in the room sounder as if it was thundering outside.

Web sucked on his wife's glorious tits that bounced with ever pump as she was letting loose a series of ecstatic cries as they both reached an orgasm.

The sex lasted forty-five more minutes before they went to the shower for part two as R. Kelly played in the background.

*****

San Fernando, Venezuela

Elena had to relocate after everything that's been going on, especially after Web kidnapping her daughter. She thought Teresa was safe. She always kept her safe since a baby and now she hated herself for bring her daughter into this.

Elena had Ariana locked in the basement in a large human dog cage with bars. She wished she could kill her but she knew that will only sign her daughter's death warrant. She knew she had to come up with a plan quick or her daughter's life would be at risk.

If Elena would've known her daughter's life was at risk, she would have let Flaco go to war alone with Web.

She been calling him to get no answer. She wanted to tell him her daughter was kidnapped, and it was his fault.

There was a knock at the door, which startled her

"Yes," she yelled sitting on her bed in a mesh gown, exposing her nice perky breast and phat shaved pussy that niggas would die for it they had a piece.

"You may want to come downstairs to see this boss, it's bad," one of her guards said leaning his head into her room to see her private parts exposed as always.

"This better be good," she said putting on her red bottom heels walking out her room in a mesh gown as her ass cheeks bounced with her sexy strut.

Once downstairs, twenty-seven guards surrounded the bag with Flaco's head cut off on top of it

"Holy shit. Get that shit out of here," she said holding her heart as if she was about to have a heart attack, but she was just shocked. "Who sent that?" she yelled as her capo handed her a small paper that said, "checkmate bitch."

Elena was pissed. She saw a couple of the guards staring at her body

"Clean it up. Don't watch me and I want that little thumb finger cut off right now. I got something for Web," she said heading back upstairs.

She knew by cutting off one of Ariana's fingers, she would get Web's attention, letting him know she was serious.

Chapter Twenty-Eight
White Plains, NY

Jamika was at work and she felt pains in her stomach, so she just left the building for an ill day because she wasn't feeling good.

She planned to stop at a store near her home to get a pregnancy test because she missed her period.

Not to mention her and Murda been having unprotected sex. She told him about this many times but once that good dick got in her, all she wanted was more.

Murda been spending a lot of time with her. When he went out of town for a week, Jamika missed him dearly as if she knew him forever.

She never felt a connection like this to no person except him. That's what made it so special to her.

Jamika even deleted Live's case out of the central files and she exposed the fact that there were eight other prints of the shells and bullets. Then she added the evidence that she hid out in the start, which was there were different bullet shells in all of the victims except two out of five victims that were murdered that night in co-op city.

Once Jamika got in Brooklyn, she picked up a pregnancy test and brought it home with her.

Thirty minutes later, Jamika was pacing around her kitchen waiting on the test results as she kept peeking at the test on the table.

She didn't know if she wanted to be pregnant or didn't, but she was raised in a Christian household and abortions were a big sin. She totally against killing babies growing inside of you.

Jamika grabbed the test that read positive.

"Yes? Oh no, no, no," she said jumping up and down then sitting down thinking about her career, the baby's mother of a dangerous drug lord killer. All types of thoughts were going through her head.

She called Murda and he told her to meet him in the Bronx at his crib and she agreed.

*****

Bronx

Murda just got off the phone with Gunna who told him about how Live's body was found on a Brooklyn curb like trash.

Murda was shocked and sick because Live was family to him. He saw him grow up. He knew there was only one person behind this and that was Joe.

Since he been back in America, he hadn't even seen his pops or Jamika yet and things were getting really serious between the two of them.

Murda was honestly feeling in love with her. He just didn't want to drag her into his crazy life.

Jamika had her own key so when he heard his door unlock, he knew it was her.

"What's up, babe?" he said as she rushed past him with her Fendi coat on.

Jamika place a white tube in front of him without saying a word as he lifted it up and read positive out loud and looked at her as she had one hand on her hips tapping her foot.

"You pregnant. Come here. Thank God," he said hugging her, lifting her off her feet.

"Put me down. So, you're ok with this?" she asked seriously after hearing all the stories of how niggas would force women to get abortions, beat them up, or leave them.

"Where you want to have your baby shower?" he asked blocking out her dumb question.

"Wow. Slow down, baby. We gotta have a grown-up talk first because I don't want my child's father in jail or worse, dead. That's my main worry," she said being honest as that played in her mind daily.

"You're right but this is my life. The best I can do is slow down because now I got you and a son to live for."

"Son? How do you know it's not a girl?" she said hugging his neck as he lifted her up on his kitchen canter tabletop.

"You right sexy. Whatever it is, I'm glad to have it with you," he said kissing her thick lips.

"Um you're such a freak."

"A big ole freak," he replied as he carried her in his room to make love to her.

*****

Upper Westside, NY

Carmilla's boss flew out to New York, which was weird to her but he told her he had first class important information, so she was on her way to meet him at a hotel where they were staying.

Carmilla been staying at Web's crib re-connecting. She had something important to tell him, but things were going so well she figured it could wait.

Carmilla parked her Benz truck in the back of the hotel, away from the heavy snow covering the lot as civilians would have to dig their cars out the snow.

When she made it to room #109, she knocked once. A boss rushed and opened the door snatching her inside the room as if someone was after him.

Carmilla's mouth almost dropped when she saw a bulletin board in the room with photos of mob boss's dead and alive. Then she saw Web and Joe the Don's faces at the top and under was photos of other people she never saw.

"I figured it out Carmilla. The link to our puzzle is this guy name Web. He is the one beefing with the mafia and I believe he has dealings to some Cartels," her boss said looking at her with a big smile.

"Are you sure?"

"Hell yeah. He's very smart but deadly too. I believe but if we nail him, we will unravel a lot more trust. Hold that thought, I have to pee. I drank four cups of Starbucks coffee," he said running into the hotel bathroom.

Carmilla was dumbfounded. Her boss broke down Web's whole operation. She knew it could lead back to her then she would be in deep shit, so she had no choice.

Her boss washed his hands while yelling to her.

"So, what you think? This could be big for D.C. if the CIA isn't already on it," he said walking out the bathroom to see Carmilla aiming a 44 bulldog at him.

"You barked up the wrong tree, boss."

"What? Carmilla what has gotten into you," he stated scared.

"Web is my husband you ass. You should've researched more," she said as he slapped himself in the head

"That's why you never completed the case."

"Smart man, but I have to go get some good dick." She shot him four times in his chest then walked out.

Chapter Twenty-Nine

Brooklyn, NY

Gabby was back in New York with Tookie. She convinced him that she wanted to have the baby at home, and she had a good doctor.

At first Tookie was against it until he hollered at Murda who told him the police killing been dead dawn. It was so much killing going on in Brooklyn with his crew, the mob, the Crips and GD's the city was having the coldest winter ever.

Gabby was by herself in a Kia Stinger GT AWD on her way to see her doctor in downtown Brooklyn.

Tookie was catching up with his friend Murda updating him on all the events he told her.

Since she been pregnant, she had the taste for fast food especially, McDonald's French fries, which drove her crazy.

She drove down Nostrand Ave to see a McDonald's on the end of the block, which made her smile as she thought about to order a number two or four.

Gabby went through the drive thru to see a car in front of her and a Lincoln Town Car that just pulled up behind her. She turned up the Hasely song on the pop radio as she began to dance in her car like a true white girl.

It was Gabby's turn to place her food order in the intercom as she pulled up close to the intercom looking at the new number menu they had on the board.

Before she could even place her order, her windows shattered all over her thinking fight or flight, she hopped out busted at the three gunmen.

Gabby hit one of the men in his neck then his lower stomach while the other two took cover from the Mack 12 she was letting off that was tearing the Lincoln car into pieces.

One of the gunmen shot Gabby in her stomach but unfortunately, he took a bullet to the head from the high-power weapon.

The last gunman hid behind the trunk shooting wildly missing her with every shot until he ran outta bullets and tossed his gun.

Gabby clutched her stomach shooting at the last man closing in on him filling his body up with bullets.

Feeling as if she was about to pass out, she climbed in the Kia running over speed bumps and passing stop signs.

Gabby knew here was no way she could go the hospital after killing three men so she went to her co-worker's house a couple of blocks away who she worked with.

Demi was an older white woman who was a nurse with a square lonely life. The only love she got was from her cats.

Today she was off, so she planned to go for a walk, shopping, and feed her cats. All ten of them.

Demi heard her doorbell. She had no husband or kids so the only person it could be at four in the evening was her neighbor, who always needed to borrow something. This was why she hated living by black people, they were to needy.

When she saw Gabby at the door bleeding to death, she yelled.

"Oh my God. Come in, come on." She helped Gabby inside and laid her on her plastic covered couch to see a fresh bullet hole. "I gotta get this bullet out," Demi said rushing to grab a first aid kit, a needle, and hot water.

After twenty minutes of working on her, the bullet was out and the wound was cleaned and sewed.

"Noooo," Gabby said rushing to the bathroom. Gabby was in so much pain she couldn't move as she pulled down her pants to see blood everywhere, knowing she lost the baby. Gabby called Tookie and told him to come to Atlantic Ave right now. Sensing something wrong he asked no questions.

Walking back into Demi's living room where she was cleaning, Demi gave her a bottle of pain killers. "You're going to need these, but you're ok, Gabby. What have you got yourself into? Those gunshots I heard earlier, was that you? Gabby you should go to the police. Someone could have killed you," Demi said in the motherly voice.

“Thank you, Demi, but sorry,” Gabby said pulling out a gun, shooting Demi in her face six times then walked placing her 380 back in her thigh hostler.

Gabby walked down Atlantic Ave to see three GMC truck cruising down the block. Tookie hopped out with the moving truck when he saw Gabby all bloody.

“What happened? Are you ok? Who did this? Where are they?” he shouted holding one hand up shutting him up.

“Take me home. We’ll talk later,” Gabby said slowly climbing in the truck as he helped her then pulled off.

*****

Manhattan, NY

Web Lounge was full and popping tonight. There was a lot of NBA basketball stars in the building for the weekend all-star game at the Barclay’s Center in Brooklyn.

Web was in his office zoned out starring at the thumb of his daughter, he received today in the mail.

There was no doubt in his mind it was his daughter’s thumb, but Web knew his next move could be his daughter’s last.

Web made a call and told his goons to have fun with Teresa, just don’t kill her. They could rape her until the moon fell from the sky.

He was going to play Elena’s game right with her because there was only enough room for one King on his throne.

*****

Venezuela

Ariana saw there was only two guards in the basement tonight. Normally there was five to six dailies.

She had her arms leaning through the bars, seeing the basement door was now open as the other guard must of went upstairs to use the bathroom.

"Guard, excuse me. Come here, sexy," Ariana said in Spanish as the chubby guard walked over to her.

"What?"

"Let me suck you off, papi. I'm so horny," she said in Spanish.

"Huh?" the man said looking around moving closer to the gate about to pull out his dick.

Ariana grabbed the man by his neck and crushed his windpipe like an apple as she grabbed his keys from his waistline.

Ariana unlocked herself out the cage and took the man's assault rifle, which was an AB-7.

She was still in her army uniform and combat boots as she walked up the stairs. She had no clue where she was.

When she made it to the top step, she saw a door leading into the kitchen where she heard voices. She looked through her small box glass window to see four guards talking in Spanish drinking liquor.

Ariana saw a backyard with woods. She knew it was her only way out alive, and she was an expert in dark woods. She was a GPS at night.

Ariana knew she was in San Fernando, Venezuela because she overheard the guard talk days ago, not knowing she was Spanish.

Ariana busted the door open and shot all four men at the speed of light, all head shots.

She heard guards running from all over the house. She made her exit at the back door and slipped off into the woods.

As she made it to the woods, shots were fired from behind her. She stopped ducked and shot forty rounds at them killing over twenty of them.

When she saw it was a clear opportunity to run, she ran in the dark woods with the assault rifle, feeling free.

Chapter Thirty

Manhattan, NY

Joe was just entered the lower garage area of his apartment complex in the city. Most of his guards waited in the garage area until he was ready to leave while two came upstairs with him.

"God damn. It's my fucking lucky day. Listen tomorrow make sure you have these dumb muthafuckers fix this elevator. This is my third time having to take stairs. I'm an old man," Joe told both of his goons as they walked towards the stairwell.

The stairwell was dark and cold as they made their way to the seventh floor. When they made it to the fourth, Joe was out of breath.

"I need a break," Joe said.

"I got one for you," Gunna said kicking the fourth-floor doorway open shooting before any of his men, as they rolled down the stairs as Joe thought he seen a ghost.

"You fucker. You want make it out this building, cocksucker?" Joe spat.

Gunna laughed as shots could be heard going off in the garage.

Knowing Joe rolled in packs, Gunna bought a sixteen-man crew for the party. When Joe heard shooting, he knew he was fucked hard.

"You remember the movie Godfather? What Mikey say when he killed his brother?" Gunna asked

"I don't fucking no kid. Do I look like the Godfather? I'm from Brooklyn, you bastard," Joe shouted before Gunna shot him nineteen times then ran downstairs towards the garage where Tookie and his crew were awaiting him.

*****

Venezuela

Elena was pissed when she came home yesterday to see half of her guards were dead and Ariana escaped.

Now she was in a fucked up situation. She was sitting by the pool sick getting a tan, when one of her guards brought her a medium box from USPS that he had to sign for.

"What you order some shoes or them Zane or Cum For Me books you like?" her capo said in Spanish as he dropped the box in front of her.

"Why don't you mind your fucking business?" she said taking off her designer sunglasses.

Elena opened the extra sealed box to see the most gruesome thing she ever saw. Teresa body was disposed and chopped up in pieces as her head was placed in the middle neatly like a turkey dinner.

Elena cried like a baby non-stop as she screamed unable to bare he lost of her daughter.

*****

Florence, Italy

Chelsea told all of Donvito's guards to take the evening off. She wanted to spend time alone with her pops.

Donivito was in his bed, high off of pain meds but still aware of his surroundings and family.

"Daddy," Chelsea stated walking in her father room to smell cigar smoke.

"Hey baby."

"How was your day?"

"Good baby. Have a seat."

"I brought a soup for you," Chelsea said sitting next to her pops who looked sick and tried.

"Thank you," her said eating her tasty soup.

"Father, I have a lot of plans for this family. You've done a good job raising us papa and I thank you."

"Chelsea, I tried to raise you good, but you got demons in you baby. You have no loyalty for family or yourself. That will be your downfall," he said in his raspy voice eating soup.

"I don't understand. I think your dose of pain meds are too high," Chelsea said with a light laugh.

"No, Chelsea you poisoned this soup. I taught you that I only blame myself. You kill your own father just to get to the top," Donivito stated.

"You're already dead, father. I'm just speeding up the process," she said.

"You believe in karma?" Donvito said still eating the soup looking at here.

"Yes."

"Good. It's a cold world. Trust no one because as you see, the closet ones to you will kill you," he said as he started to cough and choke.

"That's why I play everyone close. So close I can hear when they sneeze," she said as she watched her father's body go into shock.

When he was dead, Chelsea called the Mobsters in Italy and informed them, she will be taking over the family and she hopes to see the at the funeral.

*****

Months Later
Abu Dhabi

Web had just got off the private GG jet landing in the most beautiful city he ever saw in his life.

Abu Dhabi had beautiful crystal-clear water, tall buildings taller than the ones in New York, foreign cars, bad bitches, expensive gold, and the whole city was fill of money.

A man called Web a couple of weeks ago informing him he needs to speak to him about something important and Web agreed.

He had no clue who the man was, nor did he care he could tell by the man voice it was serious.

The man had a new G6 jet pick Web up at a private airport landing in New York and flew him to Abu Dhabi, the city of rich dreams.

Web saw three SUV trucks parked next to a Rolls Royce limo, one he never saw before because it was a drop top limo.

There were nine Emirati men standing around with assault rifles dressed in Muslim gear.

Web hopped in the Limo and drove through the city that had beautiful Muslim women walking around everywhere with barely anything on looking extremely sexy.

Life was at it best again for Web now with Joe dead and Elena somewhere hiding. Now he could focus back on chasing millions again.

Web pulled up to a tall glass building that was the same height as the twin towers. The limo entered an underground garage where he saw all million-dollar cars Bugatti's. There were ten of them, a new Bentley, new Wraiths, new Rolls Royce and new motorcycles.

"Follow me," one of the guards told Web in a strong heavy Arabian accent.

Web followed the men upstairs as he took off his Brooklyn Nets new era hat. The elevator was a glass and gold elevator, which was crazy to Web as they got off at the last stop on the twenty-eight floor.

"Webster," a Muslim man said standing in the middle of a gold floor with gold rails on the stairs, gold vases, gold picture frames, and expensive furniture everywhere.

"Who are you?" Web asked looking at guards post up all over the house.

"Come, I'm Zayid. Welcome to my country," the man said smiling with his big beard.

"Thank for inviting me," Web said sitting down a table in a diner room area with a gold china cabinet, gold silverware, and Versace tablecloth.

"I'ma get to the point. I was a good friend of your father, Jose. I was his supplier before Rafael got jealous and killed him. I've been watching you for over twenty years and I'm very impressed. I like how you dealt with Elena."

"How do you know about Elena?" Web said trying to read Zayid to see if there was any funny business.

"I was her supplier until I recently cut her off, due to your beef I should say."

"Don't let me stop your money," Web stated.

"It's not always about money. It's about loyalty over royalty," he replied as Web agreed.

"You and your son are firm together. Stay that way. It reminds me of me and my daughters. Do you remember those federal case that was against you and Murda? Of course, you do. I got those gone at the snap of a finger," Zayid said snapping his finger.

"I can repay you."

"No thank you. I brought you out here because I have the purest dope in the world and you can see more money than you seen in your life off it. I just need you and your time" Zayid stated.

"Talk. You have my attention now."

"Good. I'm going to make you a richer man, Web trust me."

Chapter Thirty-One

Months Later...
Brooklyn, NY

Jamika was in labor today and Murda was there by her side holding her hand as she yelled, screamed, and pushed.

"Push, push, push baby. Come on, do it, push," Murda yelled as Jamika pushed.

They were having a baby boy and Murda was a proud father.

Jamika took off of work for a while since she was pregnant, and the Joe case was dismissed because everybody in the case was dead so there was no case or strong evidence to hold on to or nothing.

Gunna was still running around Brooklyn with his killers pushing the little bit of weight he had left from the last big shipment.

Tookie was still in the hood with him holding shit down, but he been cuffed up with Gabby so Murda barely seen him nowadays.

His father told him he had to go to Abu Dhabi for a reason he didn't even know, but Murda didn't trust it for some reason.

"Come on, baby."

"You push a baby out!" she yelled sweaty making him laugh. "It's not fucking funny Jamel," she yelled pushing as all the doctors and nurses as they tried to help her.

"You're close. I have his head. Keep pushing," the Indian doctor said as she pushed more.

Minutes later, they had a healthy eight-pound baby boy with his daddy colorful eyes and curly hair.

The baby had Jamika's cheeks, chin, eyebrow, and ears, which made her smile to see a little boy her.

Murda had tears in his eyes when he looked at his son. He felt something he never felt until today. He felt as if he just became a man.

"Thank you."

"No. Thank you, baby. I love you," Murda said rubbing her shoulder in her hospital gown.

"I love you more. Now what's his name?"

"Andrew. I want him to have a regular name, baby," Murda stated.

"Okay, I'm fine with that."

"Excuse me, but we have to do some tests on the baby. It's only for an hour. We just want to make sure he is one hundred percent healthy and is clear to go home," A white nurse stated as she took off her face mask.

"Okay," Jamika said kissing the baby on the head before giving little Andrew to the nurse wrapped up in a blanket.

"I'm glad Tookie ain't in here. He would have been all over that trailer trash," Murda said as the nurse walked out.

"She is nice. That's nasty and mean Jamel."

"When can we get freaky again?"

"Is that all that's on your mind?" she said sucking her teeth.

"Sometimes. You know you got that thank you come back again pussy," he said making her sore body laugh.

"I have to wait six to nine weeks so you better act like you're in prison and use that hand boy."

"A baby ain't pop out your mouth so I can use that until further notice," Murda said as she hit him with a pillow.

They talked for twenty minutes until the doctor and nurse walked back in the room with crazy looks on their faces.

"You have a baby right?" the nurse asked Murda and Jamika.

"We just gave my son to you," Murda said as Jamika face frowned.

"I put him in the baby room. He's not there. I thought I saw a black hoodie leave the room. I thought it was you," the nurse said looking at Murda's black Givenchy hoodie.

"Y'all better find my fucking son!" Jamika yelled.

"Where is the room?" Murda said walking out the room with the nurse and doctor both behind him pointing at the room for doors down from where they were.

Murda entered the room to see twelve babies and they were all white babies.

"Where was his bed?"

"At the end sir," the nurse said scared something bad just happened on her watch.

Murda made it to the empty bed to see a letter wee his son was the letter read,

Murda what's good son? I'm back you missed your shot playboy but I won't miss mine. I got your little man. I be seeing you soon tell Jamika I said hey. Stacks.

Murda punched the wall screaming at the doctor and nurse. He thought he killed Stacks that night. He didn't know how he survived.

"Is everything ok? I'ma call the police," the doctor said as Murda went in the room with Jamika.

"It was a mistake, wasn't it? Where is my son?" Jamika said looking around him. "Jamel," she cried and cried until he came to hold her. "Who?" she said knowing someone got her baby.

"A man I killed, and he knew you."

"Me?" she said crying.

"Stacks," Murda said as he gave him a crazy look and cried harder.

"You killed Stacks and he got my baby," Jamika said before everything went black and Murda yelled for help.

*****

Web was on his own private plane. Zayid offered him his G6 jet but Web declined his offer. He was a good enough host to him his two day stay.

Web made a deal with Zayid. He was his new connect and he was getting pure heroin at a low price that was unheard of, but he planned to take over the streets again.

Web also told Zayid if anything was to ever happen, his son Murda will live on his legacy and empire.

The plane ride was kind of rocky, something he wasn't used to and his pilot was a perfect driver.

"You had too much to drink up there, Emmett?" Web yelled to get no answer. Normally Emmett would say something smart over the plane loudspeaker

Web saw the panel room door open to see Chelsea step out with a gun pointed at him as she were a red hooker dress with her hair in a ponytail.

"Hey Web. How was your trip? I wondered who you came to see out here," she said standing six feet away from him

"Chelsea, good to see you too," he said regretting her didn't bring guards with him on this meeting but that was a sign of disrespect.

"You don't look scared."

"I'm not."

"Before I kill you, I want to suck your dick," she said seriously.

"Kill me first, bitch."

"I will, just like I did your brother," she said as Web rushed her, but he was too slow. She emptied the clip in his head as his body collapsed on a chair then slowly slumped to the floor.

Chelsea pulled off his pants and saw his dick, which was huge soft, and started sucking it. When she was done, she cut his dick off and drunk a bottle of wine as her personal pilot flew back to New York. She hijacked his plane she been watching him closely and his pilot so it was easy to get close to him. Chelsea toasted to herself for a new era.

To Be Continued…

Murda Season 3

Coming Soon

Submission Guideline

Submit the first three chapters of your completed manuscript to ldpsubmissions@gmail.com, subject line: Your book's title. The manuscript must be in a .doc file and sent as an attachment. Document should be in Times New Roman, double spaced and in size 12 font. Also, provide your synopsis and full contact information. If sending multiple submissions, they must each be in a separate email.

Have a story but no way to send it electronically? You can still submit to LDP/Ca$h Presents. Send in the first three chapters, written or typed, of your completed manuscript to:

LDP: Submissions Dept
Po Box 944
Stockbridge, Ga 30281

DO NOT send original manuscript. Must be a duplicate.

Provide your synopsis and a cover letter containing your full contact information.

Thanks for considering LDP and Ca$h Presents.

Coming Soon from Lock Down Publications/Ca$h Presents

BOW DOWN TO MY GANGSTA

By **Ca$h**

TORN BETWEEN TWO

By **Coffee**

THE STREETS STAINED MY SOUL **II**

By **Marcellus Allen**

BLOOD OF A BOSS **VI**

SHADOWS OF THE GAME II

By **Askari**

LOYAL TO THE GAME **IV**

By **T.J. & Jelissa**

A DOPEBOY'S PRAYER **II**

By **Eddie "Wolf" Lee**

IF LOVING YOU IS WRONG… **III**

By **Jelissa**

TRUE SAVAGE **VII**

MIDNIGHT CARTEL III

DOPE BOY MAGIC IV

CITY OF KINGZ II

By **Chris Green**

BLAST FOR ME **III**

A SAVAGE DOPEBOY III

CUTTHROAT MAFIA III

By **Ghost**

A HUSTLER'S DECEIT III

KILL ZONE **II**

BAE BELONGS TO ME III

A DOPE BOY'S QUEEN III

By **Aryanna**

COKE KINGS V

KING OF THE TRAP II

By **T.J. Edwards**

GORILLAZ IN THE BAY V

De'Kari

THE STREETS ARE CALLING II

Duquie Wilson

KINGPIN KILLAZ IV

STREET KINGS III

PAID IN BLOOD III

CARTEL KILLAZ IV

DOPE GODS III

Hood Rich

SINS OF A HUSTLA II

ASAD

KINGZ OF THE GAME V

Playa Ray

SLAUGHTER GANG IV

RUTHLESS HEART IV

By Willie Slaughter

THE HEART OF A SAVAGE III

By Jibril Williams

FUK SHYT II

By Blakk Diamond

THE REALEST KILLAZ III

By Tranay Adams

TRAP GOD III

By Troublesome

YAYO IV

A SHOOTER'S AMBITION III

By S. Allen

GHOST MOB

Stilloan Robinson

KINGPIN DREAMS III

By Paper Boi Rari

CREAM II

By Yolanda Moore

SON OF A DOPE FIEND III

By Renta

FOREVER GANGSTA II

GLOCKS ON SATIN SHEETS III

By Adrian Dulan

LOYALTY AIN'T PROMISED II

By Keith Williams

THE PRICE YOU PAY FOR LOVE II

By Destiny Skai

CONFESSIONS OF A GANGSTA II

By Nicholas Lock

I'M NOTHING WITHOUT HIS LOVE II

SINS OF A THUG II

By Monet Dragun

LIFE OF A SAVAGE IV

A GANGSTA'S QUR'AN III

MURDA SEASON III

GANGLAND CARTEL II

By **Romell Tukes**

QUIET MONEY III

THUG LIFE II

By **Trai'Quan**

THE STREETS MADE ME III

By **Larry D. Wright**

THE ULTIMATE SACRIFICE VI

IF YOU CROSS ME ONCE II

ANGEL III

By **Anthony Fields**

THE LIFE OF A HOOD STAR

By Ca$h & Rashia Wilson

FRIEND OR FOE II

By **Mimi**

SAVAGE STORMS II

By **Meesha**

BLOOD ON THE MONEY II

By J-Blunt

THE STREETS WILL NEVER CLOSE II

By K'ajji

NIGHTMARES OF A HUSTLA II

By King Dream

Available Now

RESTRAINING ORDER **I & II**

By **CA$H & Coffee**

LOVE KNOWS NO BOUNDARIES **I II & III**

By **Coffee**

RAISED AS A GOON I, II, III & IV

BRED BY THE SLUMS I, II, III

BLAST FOR ME I & II

ROTTEN TO THE CORE I II III

A BRONX TALE I, II, III

DUFFEL BAG CARTEL I II III IV

HEARTLESS GOON I II III IV

A SAVAGE DOPEBOY I II

HEARTLESS GOON I II III

DRUG LORDS I II III

CUTTHROAT MAFIA I II

By **Ghost**

LAY IT DOWN **I & II**

LAST OF A DYING BREED

BLOOD STAINS OF A SHOTTA I & II III

By **Jamaica**

LOYAL TO THE GAME I II III

LIFE OF SIN I, II III

By **TJ & Jelissa**

BLOODY COMMAS I & II

SKI MASK CARTEL I II & III

KING OF NEW YORK I II,III IV V

RISE TO POWER I II III

COKE KINGS I II III IV

BORN HEARTLESS I II III IV

KING OF THE TRAP

By **T.J. Edwards**

IF LOVING HIM IS WRONG…I & II

LOVE ME EVEN WHEN IT HURTS I II III

By **Jelissa**

WHEN THE STREETS CLAP BACK I & II III

THE HEART OF A SAVAGE I II

By **Jibril Williams**

A DISTINGUISHED THUG STOLE MY HEART I II & III

LOVE SHOULDN'T HURT I II III IV

RENEGADE BOYS I II III IV

PAID IN KARMA I II III

SAVAGE STORMS

By **Meesha**

A GANGSTER'S CODE I &, II III

A GANGSTER'S SYN I II III

THE SAVAGE LIFE I II III

CHAINED TO THE STREETS I II III

BLOOD ON THE MONEY

By J-Blunt

PUSH IT TO THE LIMIT

By **Bre' Hayes**

BLOOD OF A BOSS **I, II, III, IV, V**

SHADOWS OF THE GAME

By **Askari**

THE STREETS BLEED MURDER **I, II & III**

THE HEART OF A GANGSTA I II& III

By **Jerry Jackson**

CUM FOR ME I II III IV V

An **LDP Erotica Collaboration**

BRIDE OF A HUSTLA **I II & II**

THE FETTI GIRLS **I, II& III**

CORRUPTED BY A GANGSTA I, II III, IV

BLINDED BY HIS LOVE

THE PRICE YOU PAY FOR LOVE

DOPE GIRL MAGIC I II III

By **Destiny Skai**

WHEN A GOOD GIRL GOES BAD

By **Adrienne**

THE COST OF LOYALTY I II III

By Kweli

A GANGSTER'S REVENGE **I II III & IV**

THE BOSS MAN'S DAUGHTERS I II III IV V

A SAVAGE LOVE **I & II**

BAE BELONGS TO ME I II

A HUSTLER'S DECEIT I, II, III

WHAT BAD BITCHES DO I, II, III

SOUL OF A MONSTER I II III

KILL ZONE

A DOPE BOY'S QUEEN I II

By **Aryanna**

A KINGPIN'S AMBITON

A KINGPIN'S AMBITION **II**

I MURDER FOR THE DOUGH

By **Ambitious**

TRUE SAVAGE I II III IV V VI

DOPE BOY MAGIC I, II, III

MIDNIGHT CARTEL I II

CITY OF KINGZ

By **Chris Green**

A DOPEBOY'S PRAYER

By **Eddie "Wolf" Lee**

THE KING CARTEL **I, II & III**

By **Frank Gresham**

THESE NIGGAS AIN'T LOYAL **I, II & III**

By **Nikki Tee**

GANGSTA SHYT **I II &III**

By **CATO**

THE ULTIMATE BETRAYAL

By **Phoenix**

BOSS'N UP **I , II & III**

By **Royal Nicole**

I LOVE YOU TO DEATH

By Destiny J

I RIDE FOR MY HITTA

I STILL RIDE FOR MY HITTA

By **Misty Holt**

LOVE & CHASIN' PAPER

By **Qay Crockett**

TO DIE IN VAIN

SINS OF A HUSTLA

By **ASAD**

BROOKLYN HUSTLAZ

By **Boogsy Morina**

BROOKLYN ON LOCK I & II

By **Sonovia**

GANGSTA CITY

By **Teddy Duke**

A DRUG KING AND HIS DIAMOND I & II III

A DOPEMAN'S RICHES

HER MAN, MINE'S TOO I, II

CASH MONEY HO'S

By Nicole Goosby

TRAPHOUSE KING **I II & III**

KINGPIN KILLAZ I II III

STREET KINGS I II

PAID IN BLOOD **I II**

CARTEL KILLAZ I II III

DOPE GODS I II

By **Hood Rich**

LIPSTICK KILLAH **I, II, III**

CRIME OF PASSION I II & III

FRIEND OR FOE

By **Mimi**

STEADY MOBBN' **I, II, III**

THE STREETS STAINED MY SOUL

By **Marcellus Allen**

WHO SHOT YA **I, II, III**

SON OF A DOPE FIEND I II

Renta

GORILLAZ IN THE BAY **I II III IV**

TEARS OF A GANGSTA I II

DE'KARI

TRIGGADALE I II III

Elijah R. Freeman

GOD BLESS THE TRAPPERS I, II, III

THESE SCANDALOUS STREETS I, II, III

FEAR MY GANGSTA I, II, III IV, V

THESE STREETS DON'T LOVE NOBODY I, II

BURY ME A G I, II, III, IV, V

A GANGSTA'S EMPIRE I, II, III, IV

THE DOPEMAN'S BODYGAURD I II

THE REALEST KILLAZ I II

Tranay Adams

THE STREETS ARE CALLING

Duquie Wilson

MARRIED TO A BOSS… I II III

By Destiny Skai & Chris Green

KINGZ OF THE GAME I II III IV

Playa Ray

SLAUGHTER GANG I II III

RUTHLESS HEART I II III

By Willie Slaughter

FUK SHYT

By Blakk Diamond

DON'T F#CK WITH MY HEART I II

By Linnea

ADDICTED TO THE DRAMA I II III

By Jamila

YAYO I II III

A SHOOTER'S AMBITION I II

By S. Allen

TRAP GOD I II

By Troublesome

FOREVER GANGSTA

GLOCKS ON SATIN SHEETS I II

By Adrian Dulan

TOE TAGZ I II III

By Ah'Million

KINGPIN DREAMS I II

By Paper Boi Rari

CONFESSIONS OF A GANGSTA

By Nicholas Lock

I'M NOTHING WITHOUT HIS LOVE

SINS OF A THUG

By Monet Dragun

CAUGHT UP IN THE LIFE I II III

By Robert Baptiste

NEW TO THE GAME I II III

By **Malik D. Rice**

LIFE OF A SAVAGE I II III

A GANGSTA'S QUR'AN I II

MURDA SEASON I II

GANGLAND CARTEL

By **Romell Tukes**

LOYALTY AIN'T PROMISED

By Keith Williams

QUIET MONEY I II

THUG LIFE

By **Trai'Quan**

THE STREETS MADE ME I II

By **Larry D. Wright**

THE ULTIMATE SACRIFICE I, II, III, IV, V

KHADIFI

IF YOU CROSS ME ONCE

ANGEL I II

By **Anthony Fields**

THE LIFE OF A HOOD STAR

By Ca$h & Rashia Wilson

THE STREETS WILL NEVER CLOSE

By K'ajji

CREAM

By Yolanda Moore

NIGHTMARES OF A HUSTLA

By King Dream

BOOKS BY LDP'S CEO, CA$H

TRUST IN NO MAN

TRUST IN NO MAN 2

TRUST IN NO MAN 3

BONDED BY BLOOD

SHORTY GOT A THUG

THUGS CRY

THUGS CRY 2

THUGS CRY 3

TRUST NO BITCH

TRUST NO BITCH 2

TRUST NO BITCH 3

TIL MY CASKET DROPS

RESTRAINING ORDER

RESTRAINING ORDER 2

IN LOVE WITH A CONVICT

LIFE OF A HOOD STAR

Coming Soon

BONDED BY BLOOD 2

BOW DOWN TO MY GANGSTA

CPSIA information can be obtained
at www.ICGtesting.com
Printed in the USA
LVHW081806071022
730138LV00014B/439

9 781952 936548